Lincolnshire
COUNTY COUNCIL
Working for a better future

You've ju
Pearl doesn't ca
expectations, and s
bothered about being before
was at school, girls like Pea
the pants off me. Here's what I did
stay under their radar:

1. Avoided eye contact at all times.
2. Answered no more than one question per lesson.
3. Never, ever wore anything outlandish.

mately – because I love colour, animals and sparkly
often failed at 3. For example, in Year Eight I wore a pair of
us wooden parrot earrings on non-school-uniform day. As we
ueuing for assembly, a mean girl in my class clocked my dangling
s, burst out laughing and said, 'I *love* your earrings, Jenny?'
nd I love your *face!*' I yelled back . . . silently . . . in my head.
't y a word because I was the 'quiet one' and she was the
o e' and at school it's easy to get stuck in a role, even when
le 'oesn't suit you at all.

ar uck, Pearl is about to step out of the mean-girl role she's
pl ug her entire life. But she's scared: she's been acting tough
o l , can she really change now? And will people let her?
l's ney begins at an audition for a school play when a new
ou to the room, looks her in the eye and refuses to look
S the page and join Pearl as she discovers who she
o be. Enjoy!

Also by **JENNY McLACHLAN**

FLIRTY DANCING
LOVE BOMB
SUNKISSED

ABOUT THE AUTHOR

Before Jenny started writing books about the Ladybirds (Bea, Betty, Kat and Pearl), she was an English teacher at a large secondary school. Although she loved teaching funny teenagers (and stealing the things they said and putting them in her books), she now gets to write about them full-time. When Jenny isn't thinking about stories, writing stories or eating cake, she enjoys jiving and running around the South Downs. Jenny lives by the seaside with her husband and two small but fierce girls.

Twitter: @JennyMcLachlan1

Instagram: jennymclachlan_writer

www.jennymclachlan.com

STAR STRUCK

JENNY McLACHLAN

BLOOMSBURY
LONDON OXFORD NEW YORK NEW DELHI SYDNEY

Bloomsbury Publishing, London, Oxford, New York, New Delhi and Sydney

First published in Great Britain in March 2016 by Bloomsbury Publishing Plc
50 Bedford Square, London WC1B 3DP

www.bloomsbury.com

BLOOMSBURY is a registered trademark of Bloomsbury Publishing Plc

A CIP catalogue record for this book is available from the British Library

ISBN 978 1 4088 5613 0

Typeset by RefineCatch Limited, Bungay, Suffolk
Printed and bound in Great Britain by CPI Group (UK) Ltd, Croydon CR0 4YY

1 3 5 7 9 10 8 6 4 2

For Mum and Dad . . . again and always.

*'Here's much to do with hate,
but more with love'*

CALLING ALL LOVERS
(NO HATERS, PLEASE)

AUDITION FOR *Romeo and Juliet* ...
THE MUSICAL!

AFTER SCHOOL,
MONDAY OCTOBER 11TH,
THE DRAMA STUDIO

ONE

I draw green daggers stuck deep in each heart and then I cover the poster with glittery blood. Just as I'm adding Romeo (dead), the door to the head teacher's office flies opens and Carol sticks her head out.

'Mrs Pollard will see you now, Pearl.' She peers at the noticeboard. 'Oh dear. What are you doing?'

'Nothing,' I say, dropping the pens in my bag and following her inside. Carol is Mrs P's secretary and that means we get to hang out together a lot. I grab a couple of Mint Imperials from the bowl on her desk then wander through to Mrs P's office.

My head teacher is sitting on her big swivel chair, her head bent over the pile of letters. 'Hello, Miss!' I say. She doesn't look up so I make the steel balls on

1

her executive toy start clanging against each other. Her hand shoots out and silences them. 'I've come to get my phone.' I can actually see it sitting on the corner of her desk.

She signs another letter. 'Take a seat, Pearl.'

I drop down in my usual place on the sofa. My fingers are itching for my phone. 'C'mon, Miss. I could be on Instagram right now.'

She signs a final letter, puts the lid on her pen, then looks up. 'Pearl, can you explain why Mr Hickman confiscated your phone during geography?'

'Because he's *insane*. Seriously, he totally overre-acted. I just got it out to check the time and he grabbed it off me!' I rub my hand as if it still hurts. 'He might actually have a problem . . .'

'Well, your stories don't *quite* match.' Mrs P peels a Post-it note off my phone. 'He says, "I took this off Pearl Harris because she was using it to sell the contents of my classroom on eBay."' She looks at me over the top of her specs. 'Is this true?'

'No!' I say, outraged. It's not entirely true. I'm also

selling his car. 'I think he was in a mood because he was behind with our reports.'

'What?' Her eyes narrow.

'He hadn't even started them, so he put on *The Day After Tomorrow* and did them during the lesson.' Mrs P drops the Post-it and attacks her keyboard. 'You're clearly busy,' I say, 'so how about I grab my phone and promise never to get it out in lessons ever again?'

She glances up. 'How many times have you sat there and promised me that?'

I let my head roll back and stare at the ceiling.

'Sit up,' she snaps.

'Hang on,' I say. 'Still counting.' I look at her. 'One hundred and twenty-three times?'

'Very funny.' She frowns, but the corner of her mouth lifts for a moment. I love making Mrs P laugh. Along with getting sent out of lessons, it's probably my main hobby. 'You may have your phone back tomorrow, Pearl.'

'How about *today*?'

'Tomorrow.'

'Or today might be better: like, right now.' I slowly reach for my phone.

'Oh no you don't.' She pulls it back.

I start to feel hot. All the windows are shut and the room smells of coffee and egg sandwiches. 'Miss, I *need* my phone.'

We stare at each other. Suddenly, everything about her annoys me: her little gold glasses, the way her orange lipstick has gathered in the corners of her mouth like baked bean sauce, and her owl earrings. I *despise* those owls. She takes off her glasses and pinches her nose between two fingers. The owls shiver. 'You *want* your phone, Pearl. There is a difference. Tell me why you *want* your phone so much.'

'Basically it's my watch,' I say, pulling my sleeve over my black Casio. 'Without it, I'll be late for things, like the *Romeo and Juliet* auditions that I'm supposed to be at *right now*.'

'You're a talented young lady, Pearl – clever, music-ally gifted, confident –'

'Cheers, Miss!'

'*But* I'm starting to get worried about you.' She taps her pen on the desk. 'You're at the start of Year Eleven. In a matter of months you will be sitting your GCSEs, but you're truanting, you never do homework and you have so many detentions I can't keep up with them. You're predicted A grades, but we know that's never going to happen.'

I roll my eyes. I am *so* bored of this conversation.

'Stay with me, Pearl!' she says, clicking her fingers. 'Do you remember when I met you in Year Seven? You had won a spelling competition and you came to collect your prize.'

'The Toblerone,' I say. It was a metre long. I ate half of it and put the rest in Mrs Bradman's exhaust pipe.

'You were so proud. But soon the detentions began, followed by suspensions . . .'

I make my eyes go wide. 'I promise to change, Miss.'

Her eyes flick over my skinny trousers and battered

ballet pumps and rest on my leather and silver wrist cuffs. 'Well, if you don't . . .' She pauses.

'Then what?'

'Then I won't let you be in *Romeo and Juliet*.'

I laugh. 'You wouldn't do that.'

'Yes I would. I've already spoken to Ms Kapoor. I'll do anything to keep you in school.'

I stare at Mrs P as I try to imagine not performing in *Romeo and Juliet*. I've starred in Ms Kapoor's musicals since Year Seven and I love everything about them: the dancing, the singing, the feeling I get when I walk on to the stage and everyone gazes up at me, waiting to see what I will say or do next . . .

No. I push the thought away. Mrs P wouldn't do it to me: how many times has she threatened to chuck me out of school or send me somewhere else? But here I am, still sat on this sofa while she has a go at me. 'I'd better get to the audition,' I say, standing up.

'Hang on.' She holds up one finger. 'There's something I've been meaning to ask you.'

'What?'

'Did you and Tiann steal Ms Higginson's gel pens?'

'Is that what she said?' I pick up my bag. The pens rattle around inside. 'Absolutely not, Miss. She is such a liar.'

Mrs P shakes her head and goes back to her letters. 'Come and get your phone tomorrow morning.'

At the door, I pause.

'Yes, Pearl?' she says with a sigh.

'I *need* to be in the show,' I say.

Mrs P smiles then bends her head back over her letters, owls jiggling. I leave her office, making sure I shut the door behind me.

'Everything sorted?' Carol asks.

'Great!' I start to straighten up the photos of her Jack Russell. 'How's Pippa's tick problem?'

'Much better, although I did pull a whopper off her last night.' I encourage Carol to go on about tweezers and surgical spirit then I remind her it's time for Mrs P's chamomile tea. 'You're such a thoughtful girl,' she says,

7

flicking on the kettle. Soon she's heading for Mrs P's door carrying a steaming mug.

'Oh, Carol,' I say. 'I left my phone on Miss's desk. Will you grab it for me?'

'Of course!'

TWO

I walk into the drama studio, my phone in my hand, and immediately everyone turns and stares. I have this effect on people at school. I'd like to think it's my gorgeous face . . . but more likely it's my reputation. I've done a few things in the past that people never seem to forget.

Well, let them stare. I like it. I lift my chin up, smile and look right back at them. One by one they look away, but a short girl with glasses can't take her eyes off me. Her mouth is hanging open and she's holding a crisp in the air. 'What flavour?' I ask, looking down at her.

'Smokey bacon,' she whispers.

'Nice.' I snatch it out of her hand and stick it in my

mouth. Over by the stage, my friend Kat is strumming away on her ukulele. 'See ya,' I say to the girl.

'Bye . . .'

Kat's sitting on the floor, legs crossed, back perfectly straight. I drop down next to her and she glances up, still playing her ukelele. 'What did you say to Bus Kelly?' she asks.

'Who's Bus Kelly?'

'That girl you were just talking to. You've been getting the bus with her for years.'

'Have I? I don't recognise her . . . Don't worry. I was just being friendly.' I slap my hand across the strings of her uke to stop the strumming.

She stares at my hand. 'That wasn't very friendly.'

'The thing is, Kat, when you play that thing, I want to smash it up.'

She starts playing even louder and faster. 'How about now?'

I laugh. 'Yep. Definitely want to smash it up. On you.'

She grins and strums the uke in my face until I grab it off her. 'Where are the others?' I ask. 'The others' are

Bea and Betty, Kat's friends. They used to be my friends too, back in primary school, but then we fell out. My big mouth might have had a tiny bit to do with that . . . Recently, the four of us have been hanging out together again. It's nothing like it used to be, but at least we're talking.

'They've got art catch-up. Betty's papier-mâchéing Bea's nose . . . or maybe it's her toes. Definitely some part of her body.'

'Such freaks,' I say, shaking my head.

'Hey, you promised to be nice to them.'

'I'm trying, but they make it so hard for me. Especially Betty. Is she wearing her bowler hat?'

'Yep. Don't you dare say a word about it.' Kat puts her ukulele away in its case. 'I'm guessing you want to be Juliet?'

'Want to be and *will be*. Look around you.'

'What?' She peers across the studio.

'Except for me, every girl in this room is weird, ugly or a skank. Look at Evie Russell. She manages to be all three! No way are any of them Juliet.'

'What about me?'

'You're not auditioning, are you?' That wouldn't be good. Kat actually looks quite Julietish with her big blue eyes and blonde hair.

'No,' she says. 'Too scared of you. Everyone knows it's your part. Plus there's the little issue of me not being able to sing.' She pulls a packet out of her bag. 'Jaffa Cake?'

I take four. I'm starving. 'Evie's sitting with Hairy Jonah,' I say, nibbling round the edge of a Jaffa Cake. 'Imagine if they had kids . . . they'd be *beasts*.'

'You're kind of obsessed with Hairy Jonah.'

'I am not!'

'Didn't you go out with him?'

I roll my eyes. 'For two weeks . . . over a year ago. Doesn't even count. Anyway, shut up about Hairy Jonah.'

'You're the one who can't stop talking about him.'

'I said, *shut up*!' I throw one of my Jaffa Cakes at her.

But she just laughs and says, 'Someone's feeling nervous.'

'Nope,' I say, holding out my hand. 'Totally steady.'

She stares at my fingers. 'They're shaking, Pearl.'

'That's only because I want a fag.'

'You should stop smoking – you managed it in Sweden.' Kat and I went to Sweden last summer and Kat's crazy auntie forced me to stop smoking, but the moment our plane landed in England I lit up again. Just thinking about smoking is making my hands twitch. 'Don't you want to know which part I'm auditioning for?' asks Kat.

'Go on then.'

'A man. I don't care which one. Betty says the male characters will be trained in stage combat, so we're all going to be men and fight each other!'

'Well, I'm going to be Juliet so I can be trained to get it on with Jake Flower.'

Kat stares up at the stage. 'Hello, speaking of *The Flower* . . .'

I follow her gaze. Jake's just walked on to the stage with Ms Kapoor. Everyone knows he's going to be Romeo even though Sixth-Formers aren't supposed to take part. He's such a legend he didn't even have to audition. He has his own rules at school, just like me. We'd be perfect together.

Kat sighs dramatically. 'Even his teeth are sexy . . . Have you noticed?'

'Because of the little gap?'

'That's it! And his ears . . . I like his ears.'

'His *ears*?'

She shrugs. 'I like his ears,' she says. 'Is that weird?'

'Yes. And haven't you forgotten Leo, your *boyfriend*?'

'He's eight hundred miles away in Stockholm, and right now Jake is eight metres away . . . There's no harm in looking.' We fall silent and take a moment to appreciate Jake, although Kat might be thinking about her boyfriend. She's smiling at nothing, which usually means she's drifted back to last summer and Leo.

Up on the stage, Jake is laughing, one hand messing up his short dark hair. I don't think I've ever seen him look worried. That's one of the reasons I like him so much. When I'm around him, I get this feeling that everything's going to be OK. 'Kat,' I say, 'do you remember Year Nine when Miss Butler asked us if we could think of any other words that meant beautiful?'

'And I said, "Jake Flower!"'

'You're such an idiot,' I say, but I'm laughing. 'Well, the good news is, he's just dumped his ugly, dumb girlfriend, Ella.'

'Do you mean his *stunning, clever* girlfriend, Ella?'

'Whatever. If I'm Juliet, Jake will have to kiss me – every night. We'll have to rehearse it!'

'Nice.' Kat nods appreciatively.

'Romeo!' I gasp, sticking my tongue into the jelly bit of my Jaffa Cake. '"You kiss by the book."'

'Not nice. Disgusting.'

Ms Kapoor claps her hands. 'Everyone up on the stage!'

I shove the rest of the Jaffa Cake in my mouth and point at my face. 'Juliet,' I say.

'If you say so,' she says, pulling me to my feet.

THREE

Ms Kapoor waits, arms folded, until everyone is silent. She's tied her hair back with an elastic band and, as usual, she's wearing her brown trousers with the hole in the side and the droopy hem. Ms Kapoor is such a tramp, but I love her. She's my favourite teacher.

As she tells us about our rehearsal schedule and the performances, the jittery feeling in my stomach starts to fade. It feels good to be sitting up here on the stage. Right now, the studio is blacked out and the lighting rig is arranged so that we're all bathed in a golden glow. I glance across at Jake and catch his eye. He winks at me and I smile before looking away.

'So what happens in *Romeo and Juliet*?' asks Ms Kapoor. Then her voice drops to a dramatic whisper. 'I want you all to imagine "Two households, both alike in dignity, in fair Verona, where we lay our scene" . . .'

'*What?*' says Evie.

Ms Kapoor ignores her and carries on. 'Imagine two great families, the Montagues and the Capulets, battling for supremacy in the same city. Then, one fateful day –'

'Miss,' says Evie. '*What* are you talking about? Use English.' Ms Kapoor sighs and scratches the side of her nose. It's what she always does when she's about to lose it.

'God, Evie,' I say. 'Listen, Romeo is this boy and he *says* he's in love with a girl called Rosaline, but he only wants to get it on with her – you know, like you and Harry Musham last Friday behind Iceland . . .'

Evie looks indignant. 'Sainsbury's!'

'But then Romeo goes to this party, sees Juliet and – *bam!* – they fall in love.'

'What about the other girl?'

'Rosaline? Forget her. She's not important. She's just there to show that Romeo feels *true* love for Juliet. Right, Miss?'

She nods. 'Once again, Pearl, you've stolen the stage. Carry on.'

'Romeo and Juliet's families hate each other, so they marry in secret and, get this, she's only *thirteen*.'

'OK, thank you, Pearl,' says Ms Kapoor.

'Hang on.' I hold up my hand. 'Juliet's dad doesn't know she's got married and he says she has to marry his friend, Paris. To get out of it, Juliet pretends to be dead. Trouble is, Romeo doesn't get told she's faking it and when he sees her lying there in a tomb *acting* dead, surrounded by corpses, he freaks out and drinks poison. Juliet wakes up, sees really-dead Romeo and stabs herself.' I plunge an imaginary blade deep into my guts. '*Urrghh!* Two dead teenagers – the families agree to stop fighting – the end!' Jake leads a round of applause. 'Did I remember everything?' I ask Ms Kapoor.

She nods. 'Thank you, Pearl.'

'No worries.' I might hate Ms Higginson, but she's a good English teacher. I know everything that happens in *Romeo and Juliet*.

'We're sticking to Shakespeare's original language,' says Ms Kapoor, 'just cutting some lines and a few scenes, and adding songs and dances, of course. Our very own Mr Simms has written the score. He's basically ripped off massive hits, so I'm fairly confident this show is going to rock the pants off anything we've done before.'

She grins and looks round at us before carrying on. 'We're taking over the theatre in town in the week running up to Christmas, so it has to be a totally professional show. I'm looking for the very best performers for each role.' Her eyes rest on me for a second. 'Ready for the auditions?' she asks. I am so ready. 'If you want to be Juliet,' she says, 'stay on the stage.'

'Good luck,' says Kat as she gets to her feet.

'Don't need it,' I say, looking around. The stage is almost empty: just me and a few Year Nine girls.

'Right, who's first?' asks Ms Kapoor. 'Jake's been cast as Romeo so you'll be auditioning with him.' I jump to my feet, walk to the centre of the stage and stand opposite Jake. The other girls stare up at me.

'Hello,' I say to Jake, tucking my hair behind my ear.

'Hey, Pearl,' he says with a smile. I love how tall he is. He's wearing an undone shirt, sleeves rolled up, with a white T-shirt underneath. I find myself wondering what it would feel like to slip my arms round his waist and rest against him, to have his arms wrap tight round me. 'What are you thinking about?' he asks.

I smile, not taking my eyes off him. 'Just thinking that I've not seen you out much recently.'

'Been studying . . . playing football. Why? What have I missed?'

'Me!' I say. This makes him laugh.

'Alright, you two,' says Ms Kapoor, putting a script in my hands. 'The rehearsal hasn't actually begun yet. Read these lines. It's the scene where Romeo and Juliet first meet. Remember, it's love at first sight: fireworks, pounding hearts – that kind of thing.'

'We can do that,' says Jake, nodding.

My heart speeds up and I stand a bit taller. 'Great,' laughs Ms Kapoor. She steps back, leaving us alone in the middle of the stage.

A spotlight shines down on the two of us and everyone drifts into the shadows. Jake reaches forward and takes my hand. His fingers are warm and strong. '"If I profane with my unworthiest hand",' he says, '"this holy shrine," –' his eyes flick from the script to my face – '"the gentle sin is this".' As he speaks, he pulls me so close that I can smell the fabric conditioner on his T-shirt.

'"Good pilgrim,"' I say, gripping his fingers, '"you do wrong your hand too much".' I can tell from the hush that falls across the room that everyone is watching us and, as I carry on with my lines, I feel all eyes – Jake's, Ms Kapoor's, even the other wannabe Juliets – focusing on me.

'"Move not, while my prayer's effect I take",' says Jake, pulling me even closer until our faces are almost touching, then he pauses. The script says '*He kisses her*', and now I'm holding my breath, waiting to see what he will do. He grips my hand tight and stares into my eyes.

A sudden bang echoes round the hall, making us

jump apart. Jake lets go of my hand and we look towards the door that's been thrown open. Someone is standing silhouetted in the doorway. I shade my eyes so I can see who's interrupted us. It's just some girl. She lets the door swing shut then walks towards us, stepping round students and abandoned bags. 'Who's that?' Jake whispers in my ear.

I shrug. 'Never seen her before.'

The girl stops at the foot of the stage and looks up at us. 'Hi,' she says, smiling.

I laugh. I just can't help it. Her hair is bubble gum pink and cut in a messy bob. Her dark almond-shaped eyes blink into the bright light. She's wearing weird jeans, a baggy grey sweatshirt and a My Little Pony toy is hanging round her neck. I hide my smile behind my script, but too late. Her eyes have already flashed on to me.

Ms Kapoor steps forward. 'Are you here to audition for *Romeo and Juliet*?'

She nods, still looking at me. 'I want to be Juliet,' she says.

FOUR

The girl jumps on to the stage like she owns it and I see chunky soled trainers peeking out from under her jeans. 'I thought I was going to be too late,' she says. Her accent is strange, hard to place. Part London, part American . . . and part something else.

'We've just started,' says Ms Kapoor. 'Are you new?'

'I'm starting in Year Eleven tomorrow. Mrs Stone was showing me round and told me about the show and I thought, *why not? Romeo and Juliet* is my favourite play.' She puts both her hands in her back pockets and looks around. Everyone is staring at her, but she doesn't seem at all bothered.

'Well, great!' Ms Kapoor's eyes light up. She loves anyone who's a bit different – it's one of the reasons she likes me – and this girl is *different*. Her clothes, her accent, her dark eyes. She's totally and utterly different.

The new girl bounces on her toes and says, 'I love acting and singing –'

'Where are you from?' I interrupt.

She looks back at me. 'Japan. Tokyo.'

'How come you've moved here?'

She shrugs. 'I'm staying with my dad. He's English.'

'So you've just moved all the way from Japan to live with your dad?'

'Come over here,' says Ms Kapoor quickly. 'You can watch the end of Pearl's audition.'

'Shall we start from the beginning?' I ask.

'No, carry on from where you were. Skip the kiss.'

Jake and I read on, but now we're standing apart, hands hanging by our sides, and all around us people are talking. Somehow that girl has ruined everything. Only Ms Kapoor still watches us closely, a finger pressed to her lips. 'Pearl?' says Jake.

Quickly, I say my last line. '"You kiss by the book."' Jake's already turning back to the first page of the script.

'Great.' Ms Kapoor gives her folder a light clap. 'I don't need to hear you sing, Pearl. I know you can belt them out. Now, who's next? Let's have Grace, Bethany, Jaz and then, sorry,' she says, looking at the new girl, 'what's your name?'

'Hoshi,' she says.

'We'll finish up with Hoshi.'

Without looking at the new girl, I jump off the stage and go and sit with Kat.

'That was surprising,' she says, offering me another Jaffa Cake. I push the packet away. She shrugs and we turn back to the stage and watch as Grace blushes her way through her audition. She's followed by a couple of awkward performances from Bethany and Jaz. Ms Kapoor gets each of them to sing the start of 'Let It Go'.

'Hey.' Kat nudges me as Jaz starts to sing. 'Stop looking so miserable. You were *amazing*. You and Jake leapt into each other's arms.'

'But how good is *she*?' I hiss. Up on the stage, the new girl is silently reading through her script, mouthing the words.

Kat shrugs. 'I guess we're about to find out.'

'What a freak . . . Have you seen her necklace? She's wearing *a toy* round her neck.'

'Japanese street fashion,' Kat says, nodding. 'I've got a Pinterest board on it –'

'Shh! The freak speaks.'

'She's got a name.'

'Poshi . . . Goshi . . . Noshi?'

'You know what her name is.'

Hoshi, I think. *Hoshi*. Her name makes me shiver. Up on the stage, she's still frowning at her script. Then she puts it on the floor. 'Ready,' she says, turning to Jake. He looks back at her, eyes wide. His smile has vanished.

'Your line is first, Jake,' says Ms Kapoor.

'Right. Yeah.' His eyes flick down to his script. '"If I profane with my unworthiest hand this holy shrine" . . .' He reaches his hand out to the new girl, just like he did with me, but she just ignores him and takes a step back. Jake steps closer, saying his next line, and she twists away from him, strolling to the edge of the stage. Jake follows her like a dog.

'What is she *doing*?' I say to Kat.

'I don't know, but it's funny.'

It *is* funny. She starts to say her lines – somehow she's memorised them – and all the time she's avoiding Jake's touch. People start to laugh. This makes Jake try harder and the laughter gets louder. Now he knows what she's doing, he's really getting into it.

But I'm not laughing. I stare hard at the new girl, watching every move she makes. What she's doing is so much better than what I did, it's like she's doing it on purpose. I'm glad it's dark down here. I don't want anyone to see my face.

I'm so focused on her that I don't notice Bea and Betty slip into the hall. 'Who's that?' Betty asks.

Bea's staring up at the stage, her curly hair standing out against the bright lights. 'She's *good*.' She glances at me. 'I mean . . .'

I roll my eyes. 'She's *weird*,' I say. 'She's a midget, she's Japanese and she's got pink hair. *That's* what she is.' Normally, Kat would shout me down, tell me to stop being such a cow, and recently Bea and Betty have started joining in – but instead they all exchange looks. 'What?' I say. 'She *is* weird. Look at her boy jeans and her fringe. Did she cut it herself?'

Betty shrugs. 'She looks cool. I love her Trixie Lulamoon necklace.'

'You would,' I mutter. Today Betty is wearing a man's waistcoat with her bowler hat, but I can't even be bothered to say anything about it. Then I see a ukulele case slung across her back. 'Not you too!'

'We're forming a uke band,' says Betty.

I look at Bea. 'Have you got one too?'

'Thinking about it,' she says with a shrug.

'God. I suppose it was only a matter of time.' I turn away from them and stare at the stage, my chin in my hands.

The new girl and Jake have just finished their scene. 'Shall I sing?' she asks Ms Kapoor. Then she stands at the front of the stage, puts her hands behind her back and starts to sing 'Let It Go'.

Her throaty voice effortlessly fills the studio. Even though she's staring straight ahead, I can't shake the feeling that she's singing to *me*. Annoyed with myself, I look around and see that everyone is watching her, open-mouthed. Without thinking, I pull out my phone, but still her voice creeps inside me, like the burning rush of a cigarette, making my heart pound. I stare at my fingers wrapped round my phone. I can't shut out her voice. It trickles through my body from my scalp to the tips of my fingers.

Suddenly she's finished and everyone is clapping, even Kat. I must be the only person in the whole room not joining in. The new girl laps it up, her baby-face raised to the lights.

I want to slap her.

'Wow!' says Ms Kapoor, laughing. Jake leans forward and whispers something in the girl's ear. She laughs and tugs on her necklace.

'That's some voice,' Kat says, glancing at me.

'I'm getting out of here.' I jump to my feet. I actually feel sick.

'Pearl, you don't know she's got the part,' says Bea.

'Yes, I do.' I look down at them and their silence makes me think that they know it too.

'Hang around and watch us audition,' says Betty. 'You can tell us who makes the best man.' I hesitate. Betty and I have spent most of secondary school hating each other, and now, when she's nice to me like this, it takes me by surprise. 'Go on,' she says, patting the floor next to her. 'I promise you'll get to laugh at me.'

I shake my head. I can't stay here another moment watching that girl with Jake. 'I've got to get home.'

I walk straight across the studio to the fire door. Then I take one last look at the stage. Jake is talking to the new girl. She stands opposite him, arms folded, one foot tapping. As if she knows I'm watching, her eyes flick on to me.

I turn and hit the bar on the door. It swings open, revealing a muddy football pitch and a grey sky. Behind me, I can feel the warmth of the studio, but the voices and laughter push me out into the cold air and then the door slams shut.

FIVE

The dual carriageway isn't the safest way to walk home, especially when it's getting dark, but it's the quickest. I walk with my head down, hands shoved in the pockets of my blazer as the rush hour traffic thunders past.

My mind is crammed full of the new girl. Again and again, I replay her sudden appearance, how she bounced towards us . . . how she owned the stage and how her voice silenced the room. I turn my back on the traffic to light a cigarette. It tastes disgusting so I suck a Lakrisal at the same time. Leo sends me packets of them from Sweden – salty liquorice sweets that take me back to last summer the moment I tear the silver paper.

A lorry blasts past, blowing back my hair, and I start

walking again, smoke stinging my eyes, and slowly, slowly I begin to calm down.

I turn off the dual carriageway, cut down the footpath and try Mum's phone. It goes straight to voicemail. 'Mum, it's me,' I say. 'When are you coming home?' Then I'm on the track that leads towards the farm and stables, and beyond them our house. The noise of the traffic fades away, leaving an inky sky, black trees and the lit-up farm in the distance. Mum works at the stables and gets the house with her job. As she tells us all the time: it may be a dump, but at least it's free.

A single bird starts singing, loud and clear. A robin. Gran used to tell me stuff like that. The robin sings and sings, cutting through the dark, and it reminds me of the new girl. I can see it sitting high on a branch, so I pick up a stone and throw it at the tree. The bird's wings beat the air and it shuts up.

I smile. For a moment, I feel better, but then I see our house at the end of the track, dark and alone, surrounded by trees, and my smile slips away.

I put my key in the lock, twist it, and the door clicks

open. I listen and breathe as quietly as possible. 'Alfie?' I say, listening for my brother. 'Mum?'

It's stupid. She won't be back from work yet, and if she was, Ozzie would have tried to knock me over by now. Ozzie is mum's dog and the two of them basically live at the stables, and if they're not there, they're round at Heather's house. Heather owns the farm and she's rich. Well, richer than us anyway.

I step into the kitchen, turn on the light and drop my bag in the middle of the junk on the table. I find a clean mug, fill it with water and start opening and shutting cupboards. We've got hardly any food in, just ancient tins and packets that Gran left behind – marrowfat peas, crab paste, strawberry Angel Delight. Eventually I find some bagels at the bottom of the freezer.

'Alfie?' I say as I walk into the lounge. Silence. I don't bother with the overhead light. The bulb went ages ago. I pick my way round horse tack and sacks of dog food and head for my room.

Then, out of the corner of my eye, I see an orange tip glowing in the darkness and a thin curl of smoke. Water from the mug spills on my feet. 'God,' I say. 'You scared me!' I can see him now – feet up on the coffee table, head resting on the back of the sofa. He's wearing tracksuit bottoms and a vest, like he's been working out. His curly hair is wet and slicked back. 'What are you doing, Alfie?' Silence. '*Alfie!*'

'Having a fag. What do you think?'

'Why are you just sitting here in the dark?' He doesn't reply, just carries on smoking and watching me. Alfie does this. Sometimes he speaks, sometimes he doesn't. 'When's Mum home?' I ask.

He shrugs. 'I'm going out on my bike soon.' Alfie's got a trail bike that he takes through the woods. It makes Mum mad – she hates seeing the tracks churned up. 'What've you got there?' He nods at the bag.

'Bagels.'

'Give me one. I'm starving.' I look in the bag. There are only two and they've not even defrosted yet. I throw one to him and his arm shoots up and he catches it.

'Nice catch,' I say. No answer. 'I'll be in my room.'

As I'm walking down the corridor, he shouts after me, 'Say hello to your fishies!'

I pull the string up from under my shirt, find my key and unlock my bedroom door. Mum got the first lock because she said one of us was pinching stuff from her room. She was wrong: both of us were pinching stuff. Alfie got the next lock, and then me.

As soon as I open my door, I'm greeted by a hum of filters and pumps. I flick on the light to my fish tank. 'Just me,' I say, as the fish zigzag around. 'I'm back.' I put my face close to the glass and see a whirl of cartoon stripes and neon tails darting through coral and waving plants. I check each fish in turn. 'Hello, Oy,' I say to a little orange and black fish. Oy's my clownfish, my very own Nemo. He's trying to hide behind a bit of wood, but he's too bright to hide anywhere. 'Having a good day?' I ask him. He looks startled and his mouth forms a perfect 'o'.

I grab my laptop, put on Sub FM then sit in front of my tank. I go on Facebook then YouTube, clicking from film to film. I don't know what I'd do without my laptop. Dad got it for me for my birthday – a guilt present for never seeing me. He said we'd Skype on it, but that's never happened. After watching some girl vlogger make cheese on toast, I get into an argument with harry16 after he posts: **woah she so ugly!!!!**

I reply as Peawitch: **woah you so dumb!!!!**

Immediately he replies: **said the dumb ugly girl**

So I'm forced to log in as Queenyx_x on my phone – she's much ruder than Peawitch – and she says to harry16: **am watching your ugly face right now thru window & it makes me sick** . . . He tries to retaliate, but Queenyx_x and Peawitch destroy him. After posting **you guys mean** ☺ he goes quiet.

I stare at the screen. Usually, I love doing this kind of thing, but I can't get into it tonight. My mind keeps going back to the auditions and the unbearable thought that I might not be Juliet. And I think about *her*, of course, the new girl, and how everyone stared at her. How Jake stared at her.

I turn my music up then push my laptop away. Resting my chin in my hands, I watch my fish.

They always make me feel better.

Originally it was Jon's tank, some guy Mum went out with. He set it up in the dining room and every Saturday he'd take me to World of Water to buy a new fish. The garden centre has a cafe and we'd sit opposite each other, him putting sugar in his coffee and me dipping a Twix in hot chocolate, and he'd chat to the fish in their plastic bag sitting on the table between us. It was stupid stuff like, 'How rude, I didn't get you anything,' but it made me laugh.

One day I came home from school and Jon had left, but his tank stayed because it was too heavy to move. I spent so much time in the dining room, feeding the fish and cleaning the tank, Mum let me turn it into my bedroom.

Now I work at World of Water on Sundays. I suppose I've got Jon to thank for that.

There's a knock at my door. 'Pearl?' Mum sticks her head in and stares at the clothes, mugs and towels scattered across the carpet. 'God, what a mess,' she says and Ozzie's nose appears by her knees.

'The whole house is a mess,' I mutter.

'I never see you doing anything about it.' Her face is

brown and wrinkly from all the time she spends outside with the horses. I used to think she was glamorous with her curls, skinny jeans and riding boots, but these days she just lives in dirty leggings and wellies, and her hair's scraped back in a bunch. 'There's a couple of pizzas in the oven,' she says. 'Heather was defrosting her freezer and needed to get rid of them.'

'Yeah?' I realise I can smell melting cheese.

'Come and help me.'

'Is Alfie in?'

'No. He's disappeared on his bike.'

'Can we do chips?'

She thinks for a moment, then smiles. Mum's smiles don't happen very often. 'If you peel the potatoes,' she says. I jump up. Ozzie by her side, Mum treads carefully across my room to peer into the tank. 'Look at that fish.' She points at the tang, who's chasing a firefish. No matter where the tiny firefish goes, the tang is right behind it, nipping at its tail and pushing it into corners.

I can see my smile reflected in the glass. 'It's a right little bully,' I say.

SIX

The moment she sits down on the bus, Tiann shoves a locket under my nose. 'Do you like it?' she asks. 'Max gave me it last night to celebrate our four month anniversary.' I hold it between two fingers, but the bus goes over a bump and it bounces out of my hands. 'Careful!' she squeals.

'Did he nick it from Poundland?' I say. 'Because, if I'm honest, it looks a bit cheap.'

'Shut up! It's an heirloom. It belonged to his nan.'

'The one who works at Poundland?'

'Ha ha,' she says, but she's so loved up she's can't even be bothered to get annoyed with me. She caresses the gold heart on the front of the locket.

I force myself to say something nice, or at least

something not mean. 'What've you put inside?'

She uses her fingernail to prise it open. 'Look. On this side it's a photo of his eyes – amazing – and on this side it's his guns.' She kisses the tiny, blurred pictures. 'They're my favourite things in the whole world!'

I stare at her. 'Seriously? Max's *arms* are your favourite things in the whole world?'

'Yeah!' She nudges me. 'Look. Check them out.' Max has got on the bus and is making his way towards us. I can't see anything special about his biceps, but maybe that's because they're hidden inside a blue polyester blazer. Tiann leans towards me and whispers, 'He's got this vest that says, "Sun's out, guns out"!'

Now that's something I never want to see.

'Hey, babe,' Max says, and Tiann jumps to her feet and they kiss. Noisily. For ages. In Year Nine I went out with Max for a couple of days. Then I noticed his mouth tasted of ham. Tiann doesn't care. She loves ham. 'Alright, Pearl?' Max says.

'Well, I've just had to watch you two making out, but

apart from that I'm OK.' But he's not listening and Tiann's already leading him to an empty seat at the back of the bus.

I don't care about being left on my own. I need to think about the new girl. When I woke up this morning, I couldn't believe I'd let Pink Hair get to me so much and I jumped out of bed actually looking forward to getting to school and letting her know just who she's messing with.

Overnight some Shreddies and milk had appeared in the kitchen, so I ate a big bowlful then did my hair and make-up. Things got stressful when Alfie appeared and told me the Shreddies were his. I probably shouldn't have laughed because he emptied the rest of the packet over my head. I screamed. Mum woke up, screamed at both of us, and then Alfie called me a crow. Crow? Whatever. I kind of like it and it's better than slag or skank.

Anyway, I've had breakfast, my hair's big and my make-up's perfect, so the new girl had better watch out. Later, we're finding out which parts we've got and I'm sure I'll be Juliet: why would Ms Kapoor give the part to some girl she's only just met?

Just then the bus pulls up outside Tesco and the best thing happens: the new girl gets on. Immediately I sit up and watch as she shows her pass to the driver. She's wearing uniform today – a blazer that's way too big and a long ugly skirt. Her hair's still a short messy bob, but overnight it's turned white. Excellent.

The bus moves away and she wobbles and makes a grab for the back of a seat. A boy tries to sit next to me. 'Seat's taken,' I say, pushing him away. 'New girl!' I shout. She looks over. 'Sit with me.'

She doesn't know it, but I'm about to become her frenemy.

She smiles and walks down the aisle, swaying as the bus picks up speed. 'Pearl, right?' She takes the free seat.

'That's me.' I stare at her. 'What's with the grey hair, Poshi?'

'It's Hoshi.'

'Right, sorry. *Hoshi*.'

'Mrs Stone said I couldn't have it pink, so I dyed it,'

she says, running her fingers through the ends. 'Does it look OK?'

'It looks *amazing*!' I'm such a good liar. She looks like she's wearing a scraggy old Elsa wig. 'Blondes have more fun, right?'

'Right,' she says uncertainly.

I take in her scrubbed clean face and her pointed chin. The only make-up she's wearing is a flick of eye-liner above each eye. It exaggerates the cat-like shape of her eyes. 'So, what do you think of Jake?' I ask. 'You two seemed to be getting on last night.'

'Jake? The boy playing Romeo?' She shrugs. 'Nice. I mean, I didn't talk to him much.'

'He's been going out with this Sixth Form girl for as long as I can remember.'

'Yeah?' She leans back and looks at me. 'He didn't mention her.'

'They're practically married,' I say. 'I suppose he thinks everyone knows about him and Ella. Do you want me to fill you in about our school? Useful stuff to know?'

'That would be great, Pearl.' She smiles and I smile back. The whole situation is so fake I almost burst out laughing.

'OK,' I say, 'let's start with the head, Mrs P. She's got a *crazy* sense of humour. Anything goes with her.'

'Really? She seemed strict.'

'Nah. Just tease her a bit. She loves it.' For the rest of the journey, I tell her all about our different teachers. I'm not entirely truthful, but Hoshi laps it up and I really start to enjoy myself. At one point, when I'm telling her about homework, she even gets out a notepad and starts making notes with a Snoopy pencil.

'So Mr Simms doesn't care if you do homework, right?'

'Never even asks you to hand it in.' Actually, he gives out automatic after-school detentions.

'This is so different to Japan,' she says, shaking her head. 'We all have to help clean the school and we bow to our teachers.'

'No way!' I say. 'It's like the opposite here – so relaxed. You don't even have to put your hand up to

44

answer questions. Just call out. The teachers love it because it shows you're into the lesson. If you're thirsty, have a drink. Sometimes I stop off at Starbucks on my way to school and take in a mocha.'

'Really?'

The bus pulls up outside our school. 'And a lot of the teachers let us call them by their first names,' I say. 'Mrs P is cool if you call her Tara, and Mrs Stone is called Sarah.' With a hiss of the brakes, the bus comes to a stop. 'Oh, there is one thing it helps to know about Mrs Stone.'

'What's that?'

'She's pregnant.'

'I didn't realise.' Hoshi bites her bottom lip, like I've just given her too much stuff to remember.

'Couldn't you tell? She's massive!'

She frowns. 'I suppose so.'

'Anyway, she *loves* talking about it. If you want to get her onside or need to distract her, just ask if it's a boy or girl, that kind of thing. She's got total baby-brain at the moment.'

'Thanks, Pearl!' Hoshi drops her notepad back into her bag. 'I feel so much better now.'

I give her arm a squeeze. 'No worries!'

We get off the bus and walk across the playground. Mrs Stone and Mr Hickman are out on duty. 'Hi, Miss,' I say. 'Hi, Sir!'

'Morning, Pearl,' says Mr Hickman. 'Did you go and see Mrs Pollard about your phone?'

'Yes, and I'm *so* sorry about that, you know, the whole eBay thing.' Mr Hickman shakes his head in disbelief. 'What?' I say. 'I really am sorry! I was having a bad day.'

Mrs Stone's sipping her coffee and watching me and Hoshi. She doesn't look too happy seeing me hanging out with the new girl. 'Hoshi,' she says, beckoning her over, 'a word, please.' I hang around, curious to hear what she's about to say. 'What's this about?' She points at Hoshi's ball of white hair.

'You told me it couldn't be pink,' Hoshi says.

'It has to be your natural colour,' says Mrs Stone. 'You can't just dye it a different colour. It needs to be . . . black.'

'Black?'

'Or brown. What colour is your hair?'

'Blonde,' says Hoshi, her eyes wide.

'Blonde? Not . . .' Mrs Stone frowns and looks at Mr Hickman for help. He shrugs. 'Isn't your hair naturally black?'

'Oh!' says Hoshi, laughing. 'I get it. I know most Japanese people have black hair, but my dad's English. He's a blond like me.' Hoshi twirls a strand of her bleached hair between her fingers. 'This is my natural hair colour.'

This is great. No way is Hoshi blonde. Mrs Stone starts to go pink as she tries to work out what to say. 'Right,' she says, gulping some of her coffee. 'You're blonde. Fine. Well, you two had better run along to your lessons. You don't want to be late on your first day, Hoshi.'

'No way,' she says, smiling sweetly. 'Thanks, Sarah!'

'What?' Mrs Stone's eyes shoot open.

'By the way,' says Hoshi. 'I am *so* excited about your baby.'

Coffee spills on the playground. 'What *baby*?'

'Your baby.' Hoshi nods at Mrs Stone's dumpy stomach that's squeezed into stretchy beige trousers.

Suddenly, I get a bad feeling about this. 'Come on, Hoshi,' I say, trying to pull her away. 'I need to show you where your science room is.'

But she's not moving. 'Pearl's been telling me all about school and you being pregnant. When's the baby due? Not long now I'm guessing.'

Mr Hickman squints up at the sky. 'Right. I think I might get going,' he says, moving off in the direction of his classroom.

'Me too,' I say.

But before I can move a step, Mrs Stone's hand clamps round my wrist and she hisses, 'Stay where you are, Pearl Harris.'

Hoshi looks alarmed. 'Did I say something wrong?'

Mrs Stone shakes her head. 'You can go, Hoshi.'

'I'll see you later, Pearl?'

'Yeah,' I say with a sigh. 'Remember the cast list goes up before lunch.' I wriggle out of Mrs Stone's grasp and get my phone out. I like to multi-task when I'm being told off.

'Shall we say lunchtime in my office, Pearl?' Her voice is icy.

'Whatever.' For a moment, I wonder if she's going to tell Mrs P, but if I do a lot of butt-kissing during the detention I should be OK.

'Put your phone away when I'm talking to you.' I drop it in my pocket and stare across the playground. Hoshi is going into the science block. She glances back at me. Her worried frown has gone and in its place is a smile. A big smile. It could be friendly, but I just can't tell. She gives me a little wave.

'Bitch!' I whisper.

'What did you just call me?' says Mrs Stone. Her face has gone a strange colour.

OK. Now I'm in trouble.

SEVEN

'I'm Mercutio!' says Betty, peering at the cast list, her stupid bowler hat blocking my view. 'Not only is he a man, but he's the funniest man in the play *and* he dies in a sword fight.'

'Move up.' I push her aside. 'I'm supposed to be at detention.'

I see it immediately, typed out for the world to see: *Juliet – Hoshi Lockwood*. I put my finger under the words and read them again.

'Oh, crap,' says Betty. 'I'm sorry, Pearl.'

My mouth has gone dry and I feel sick, right down at the bottom of my stomach. I swallow and keep my face blank and stare at the words until they've sunk in. Ms Kapoor has written a quotation about each character on the cast list. Next to Hoshi Lockwood, it says: *Juliet –* '*She doth teach the torches to burn bright*'. Two lines down, it says: *Pearl Harris – Tybalt – 'Peace. I hate the word.'*

'It's OK,' I manage to say.

It's not OK. Right below Hoshi's name is Jake's. So close together. Romeo's quote is '*Dear perfection*'. Jake and Hoshi . . . Romeo and Juliet. *Perfection*.

'Look,' says Betty, tapping the list. 'You're Tybalt. It's such a good part. He's Juliet's cousin and he goes round fighting everybody and –'

'I know who he is.'

'You get to kill me! Total wish fulfilment, Pearl.'

I turn away from the list and look at her. Two strawberry-blonde plaits hang down from her bowler hat and she's drawn a biro flower on one of her cheeks. When we were at primary school, we had so much fun being bad together: stealing the gerbils' sunflower seeds then feeding them to Louis Benedict; telling everyone the middle toilet was haunted by a wee-ghost; putting our clothes on back to front after P.E. . . . Then we came to secondary school and suddenly we had nothing in common. Except hating each other.

'Killing you would be fun,' I say with a smile.

'There we go!' she says, laughing. 'And you're Hoshi's understudy . . . But don't push her down the stairs or lock her in any cupboards.'

We walk away from the noticeboard and immediately our places are taken by other students. 'Or under a bus?' I say. Then I grin. Betty's made me think: just because it says Hoshi is Juliet on a piece of paper, it doesn't mean it's *actually* going to happen. There are weeks until opening night and I am her understudy . . .

'Definitely don't push her under a bus. It's murder,' says Betty.

'Boring,' I say, but I'm distracted and now my mind is whirring, trying to work out how Hoshi could be kicked off the show . . . or persuaded to drop out. There are so many little things I can do to help her change her mind. Nothing too bad. Just get in her face a bit, make her realise life would be so much easier if she wasn't Juliet.

'Alright, ladies?' It's Kat. Bea's hiding behind her, eating a slice of pizza.

'Year Eleven girl eating pizza in the corridor!' shouts Betty, turning round. 'Hello? Is *no one* on duty out here? Bea Hogg is breaking a rule!'

'Shut up,' says Bea. 'I actually hate you, Betty. You know that, right?'

'You love me!' says Betty.

'Quiet, girls,' says Kat. 'I need information. Who am I?'

'Boy,' Betty says, her eyes flicking to me, checking I'm alright.

'What? *Boy?* That's not a part. What else does it say?'

'Nothing. That's it.'

'Boy?' She shrugs. 'Oh, well. I said I wanted a male role. Who's Bea?'

'Potpan.'

'That doesn't sound good,' says Bea, sticking the last bit of crust in her mouth. 'Is Potpan a person or a thing?'

'He's an unintelligent servant,' I say.

'Bum . . . It's because I can't sing.'

'Probably,' I say, then quickly I add, 'and I'm not Juliet.'

'Oh, Pearl!' Kat grabs my arm. For a moment I think she might hug me, but she thinks better of it. 'Are you OK?'

'Fine.' I shake her off. 'It's just a school musical.'

'That sucks,' says Bea, eyes wide. 'Who are you?'

'Tybalt . . . and the evil Japanese elf is Juliet.'

'Hi, guys!'

I spin round. The evil Japanese elf is standing right behind me. She can move quietly on those tiny feet. 'You're Juliet,' I blurt out.

She nods and smiles, like it's just what she expected. She looks so smug I want to shake her. 'Our first rehearsal is next week, right?'

'Monday,' says Kat.

'It's going to be fun,' she says, still smiling. Then she clocks the awkward silence and seems to remember we were auditioning for the same part. 'Who are you, Pearl?'

'Tybalt.'

'Awesome! We're going to be cousins.'

'Awesome,' I say.

The silence comes back and it's only broken when Betty gasps, 'Oh my God!' and grabs Hoshi's hand. 'Domo-kun *nails*. I love Domo-kun.' Then the two of them start talking about Domo-kun, who apparently is a Japanese cartoon character who came out of an egg and lives with a rabbit.

I glance at Hoshi's nails. Each one is painted brown with jaggedy teeth and black eyes.

'Look,' says Betty. She pulls up her blazer sleeves, revealing her own Domo-kun wrist warmers. 'I knitted these myself.'

'Can you knit me some?' asks Hoshi. 'Even better, will you teach me how to do it?'

'Domo-kun knitting party!' says Betty.

I've had enough of this. 'I'd better go,' I say. 'I'm late for my detention.'

'What did you do?' asks Kat.

'Nothing. Just Mrs Stone being a total cow, as usual.' I glance at Hoshi, but she's not giving anything away. 'Got to go.'

'*Sayonara*, Pearl!' says Hoshi, then she sticks two Domo-kun nails into a peace sign by her face and gives me her cute little smile.

'Whatever,' I say as I walk down the corridor.

At first Mrs Stone is furious, but as she's lecturing me I see a magazine called *Rock'n'roll Weddings* sitting on her desk. All I need to say is, 'Are you getting married, Miss?' and suddenly all is forgiven. Admittedly, I do have to spend ages discussing her ridiculous Doctor Who theme and browsing the internet for Dalek cakes, but at least it gets me out of trouble.

I take my time walking to science. I'm thinking tactics, trying to work out the best way to get Hoshi off the show. Problem is, I can't do anything around Kat and the others; there's this unspoken rule that I only get to hang out with them as long as I behave myself. No, I'm just going to have to be patient and get to know Hoshi better. Then, when she's least expecting it . . . I'll strike!

I'm brought back to reality by a pair of hands landing

on my shoulders. I spin round and see Jake's smiling face. 'Sorry,' he says. 'Didn't mean to scare you!'

'Well, you did,' I say, laughing.

'I've been looking everywhere for you.'

'Yeah?'

He runs his hands through his hair. 'I saw the cast list. Bad news, mate. I thought you'd be Juliet . . .' He can't quite look at me when he says this.

I shrug. 'Ms Kapoor obviously didn't think I was good enough.'

'No way. You'd be great.' Then he hits me with his smile and as usual it makes me feel so good. I love this about Jake. Even though some people look at me like I'm scum, he never does. 'Now you're Tybalt,' he says, 'at least we get to fight each other.'

'Jake, you kill me.'

He laughs. 'Do I? I'd better read the play. What happens?'

'You murder me because I've killed your best friend, Mercutio. It's revenge.'

He takes my hand, links his fingers round mine and

says in a deeply serious voice, 'Apologies in advance for having to kill you.' He squeezes my fingers then lets go.

'Hey,' I say, 'are you going to Lottie's eighteenth on Saturday?'

'Not sure.'

'I'm going,' I say. 'You should come.'

'Maybe I will . . .'

'I've got to go. I'm late for science.' I turn and walk away, but I know he's watching me, so I walk a bit taller.

'Looking forward to that fight!' he calls after me, and somehow I know he's smiling. You can feel a Jake Flower smile even when you can't see it.

EIGHT

I don't waste any time becoming Hoshi's frenemy. All week I wait for her outside her lessons and sit next to her whenever we have a class together.

Soon I know loads about her: how she loves salt and vinegar crisps and that her dad's called Ed and that she's got a thing for quirky accessories. Every day it's something different: knee-high white socks, one pulled up, the other pushed down; a ring made up of two birds kissing; an ice-cream hair grip. I tell her that I *love* her toddler look, and she just smiles and says, 'Thanks so much, Pearl!'

I ask her all the right questions, lend her a pound when she needs it, and I even start to help her learn Juliet's lines. I tell myself that I need to be patient, but it's starting to feel like I'm all friend and no enemy.

So today, just before our rehearsal, I sneaked into our English room, found her book and stuffed some Wotsits between the pages. Then I sat on it and wriggled around until it was full of cheesy dust. It was a pathetic thing to do, but at least I was doing something.

'What are you smiling about?' asks Kat as we're warming up.

'Nothing!' I say. 'Come on, you're supposed to insult me.' Miss wants to get us in an aggressive mood because the play starts with a fight. She's put on dance music and strobe lights and told us to go round the room throwing Shakespearean insults at each other.

'OK . . . "Thou art like a toad,"' says Kat, picking a phrase off the list, '"ugly and venomous"!'

'Hang on,' I say, scanning my sheet of paper. 'Kat, thou have a moustache.'

'That's not what it says,' she cries. 'Shakespeare *never* said that!'

'I made it better,' I say, my eyes flicking round, looking for Hoshi.

Kat's got a mirror out of her pocket and is poking her tongue under her top lip, checking it from all angles.

'Girls!' shouts Ms Kapoor. 'Go round the room. Insult everyone, not just your friends.' With a sigh, Kat and I separate. Ms Kapoor catches up with me. 'Forgiven me yet, Pearl?'

The music thuds and the lights flash on and off. 'Not yet,' I say. 'Give me a few years.' I'm only half joking and she knows it.

'I'm right about this,' she says. 'You'll see.' She puts a hand on my shoulder to stop me walking away. 'You're going to be the *best* Tybalt.'

'If you say so.' I smile and twist away from her. I don't really blame Miss. The person I blame is in the corner of the studio with Betty. Her black kitten ears make her easy to spot.

I'm pleased to see Jake is on the opposite side of the room to Hoshi. He never turned up at Lottie's party and it was a disaster. Tiann left early and I got a Sixth

Former to buy me a couple of drinks, then had an argument with some girl. Eventually Lottie's uncle made me leave. At work the next day I felt so sick, my boss, Jane, let me lie on a sun lounger in the stock room until I felt better. I kept pressing a cold can of Coke into my face and trying not to think about Hoshi. Somehow it all seemed like her fault.

'Get insulting, Pearl!' calls Ms Kapoor.

I (accurately) call a Year Nine boy an 'eye-offending maggot-pie' then move on round the studio. Suddenly, I find myself in front of Bus Kelly. She stares at me through her big blue specs. 'Do your worst,' I say. 'Slag me off. I can handle it.'

'Um . . .' She looks at her list.

'Yes?' I step closer and she whispers something. 'What? Can't hear you.'

'"Bull's pizzle"!' she blurts out.

'And thou,' I hiss, grabbing the front of her blazer and pulling her close, 'art a "cream-faced loon"!' She blinks up at me and I let her go. 'You know I'm joking, right?'

She nods and runs away.

Automatically, my eyes find Hoshi. She's by the stage insulting some boy. I go and tap her on the shoulder. She spins round. 'Hey, Pearl!' she says, a big smile on her face. 'Who's going first?'

'Me. I've been saving a couple for you.'

'Great.'

'You "bolting-hutch of beastliness",' I say, stepping towards her. 'You "swollen parcel of dropsies".' She takes a step back. 'You "bombard of sack". You "stuffed cloak bag of guts"!' I haven't got a clue what I'm saying, but I'm enjoying myself so much. I move forward until she's against the wall. Then I put my face close to hers and, very quietly, I say, 'You "ratcatcher".'

Hoshi stares right into me. '"Go prick thy face", Pearl,' she says with a big smile. Then she slips past me. I stand there for a moment staring at the wall, my hands clenched. Once again, she's beaten me . . . only I don't know how she's done it. My words just seem to bounce off her.

I turn round and find myself standing opposite Jake.

His eyes flick down the list, then he says, 'How are you doing, "fusty nut"?' White strobe lights flash on his face. They're making me dizzy.

'Frustrated,' I say. 'I don't like warm-ups.'

He studies me. 'What would you rather be doing, Pearl Harris?'

Music bangs out of the speakers next to us and I feel the bass deep inside me. Jake flashes in and out of the darkness. 'Actually,' I say. 'Now I think about it, this is pretty good.'

He laughs. 'Aren't you going to insult me?'

I glance at the list then say, 'You're a "notable coward". A "promise breaker".'

Just then Ms Kapoor stops the music and puts the lights on. Jake frowns. 'I'm sorry I couldn't make it to the party. I had to help my dad out at work.'

'The party?' I say. 'Lottie's? It was rubbish. I left early.'

'Get over here, you two,' calls Ms Kapoor. Everyone else is sitting in a circle, waiting for us.

Jake stands back to let me pass. For the briefest of

moments I feel his hand on my back and I imagine how we must look together: tall, dark, the *perfect* pair. On the other side of the circle, Hoshi is watching us as we take our seats. I smile at her. She may be acting Jake's girlfriend, but who's sitting next to him right now?

She rests her chin in one hand and smiles back, her eyes never leaving mine. Then her script comes up, hiding her face, and all I can see are her kitten ears poking out of her hair.

NINE

For the rest of the week, I have to watch while everyone falls under Hoshi's spell. Even the teachers seem to think she's amazing.

When Kat and I walk into the drama studio for Thursday's rehearsal, the first thing I see is Hoshi chatting to Ms Kapoor. They're going over the script, making notes, laughing. It used to be me Miss talked to before rehearsals; sometimes she'd even bring me a cup of tea from the staffroom. I feel pathetically relieved when I see there's no mug in Hoshi's hands.

'What's the matter?' Kat says, looking at me.

'Nothing.' I force myself to smile.

'Is it still bothering you?' Kat says, glancing at Hoshi and Ms Kapoor. 'Hoshi being Juliet?'

'No,' I say quickly.

'Because you've got such a good part,' Kat says, 'and this *is* just a school show. I know Ms Kapoor goes on about how life-changing it's going to be, but it'll be over in a few months.' She smiles, thinking she's said just the right thing.

I look at Kat, her blonde hair hanging perfectly over each shoulder, little diamond studs glinting in her ears. They were a present from her mum and dad for her sixteenth birthday. 'I said it's not bothering me,' I say, then I walk away. 'Come on. Let's get a seat before they all go.'

Mr Simms runs through some scales as he waits for us all to sit down, and then he starts to describe our first song. 'We're opening with a power ballad. Shakespeare didn't think of that!' He starts to play a very familiar tune, glancing back at us over his shoulder. 'I'm rather pleased with what I've written,' he says. 'It's called "Capulet It Go" and it goes like this.' He begins singing in a dramatic baritone. '"The heat burns bright in the square today, no Montagues to be seen, but with

our swords and daggers, we're ready to vent our spleen!"
What do you think?' he asks, still playing.

'It's "Let It Go" from *Frozen*, Sir,' says Evie.

His hands crash down on the keys. 'No, actually it's very different if you listen carefully.' He plays the opening of each song. 'See! Different key. Different track altogether.' I'd say they're almost identical, but who cares. It sounds great.

'You're going to get sued by Disney,' says Evie. 'They'll cancel our show.'

'Disney's never going to know about it . . . but just in case, let's say mobile phones are banned. OK?' He gives a pile of music sheets to a student and they're passed along the row. 'Everyone got the lyrics? Let's learn the song.'

I prefer solos, but it still feels good to be part of one big voice. For a while it distracts me, keeps me in the moment, but Hoshi is sitting somewhere behind me and I find I can't block out her voice. It lifts above all the others, so I work on drowning her out and Mr Simms is thrilled. 'That's it, Pearl! So much passion.'

Just as we've got the hang of the song, Ms Kapoor comes back into the studio dragging a box behind her. 'We're going to do some fighting,' she says, 'but before we do that, I want to tell you some exciting news.' She pauses and smiles. 'We're going on a trip to London!' She explains that she's been in touch with a friend at Pineapple Dance Studios and arranged a street dance workshop for us. 'It's last minute – we're going next Friday – so get your consent forms in quickly.'

'Friday,' Kat whispers in my ear as the letters go round. 'We're going to swap double maths for krumping!'

'Back to business,' says Ms Kapoor. 'The business of fighting! I've raided the props cupboard and I thought we could try singing "Capulet It Go" and do some combat improvisation at the same time.'

I decide that I've definitely forgiven Ms Kapoor. What an insane idea!

She starts throwing us weapons – wooden swords, plastic cutlasses, foam daggers. Kat gets an AK-47 and I get an inflatable axe.

'Am I meant to have this, Miss?' Bea pulls a Samurai sword out of its sheath.

'Better not.' Ms Kapoor swaps it for a plastic sabre. 'I brought that back from Japan and it's kind of real.'

'Not fair!' says Betty. Somehow she's ended up with a floppy cardboard dagger. Bea starts prodding her with her sabre, so Betty retaliates by slapping her round the face with the cardboard dagger.

'Hang on,' says Ms Kapoor. 'I don't want you to just go crazy and hurt each other. Mr Simms will accompany you while you sing. At the same time, move round the room and *gently* fight with whoever your meet – almost in slow motion. Ready?' She nods at Mr Simms. 'Go!'

For about ten seconds we fight *gently*, all the time singing 'Capulet It Go', but soon the fighting is too much fun and we abandon the singing for pure fighting. I focus on hitting Kat round the head with my axe. She's laughing so much she has to crouch down in a ball. 'Stop!' she screams. 'You're going to whack a wee out of me!'

I take pity on her and look round to see who else I can torment. Ms Kapoor is standing on a chair, looking anxious. A sword swings near her face and she pulls back, her eyes wide. 'Time out!' she yells to the small girl in front of her. 'Sit on the stage.'

Bus Kelly throws down her sword and stomps off.

Suddenly, Hoshi appears in front of me and swipes at my axe with her wooden sword. 'Ha!' she says. I take a swing at her, but she jumps easily out of the way and sneaks her sword under my arm to try and jab my stomach. I step back. 'Is that the best you've got, Pearl?' she asks, jumping from side to side. 'I've seen babies fight harder than you!' Is she trash-talking me?

'You don't want to know what I've got,' I say. Then I lay into her, my axe squeaking each time it hits her sword. Biting her lip with concentration, she goes for my left arm, then switches at the last moment, gently prodding my leg. It's a sneaky move. 'Got you,' she says. 'You're dead!'

'No.' I pull my axe back. 'You're dead!' I aim for her head, whipping the axe round hard. *Wheeeeee!* goes the axe as it slams into her fluffy hair, and it's so satisfying. For a moment, Hoshi blinks and rocks backwards, her hair sticking up all over the place. 'Head rush,' she says, smiling.

Ms Kapoor is not amused. 'Pearl!' she shouts. 'Too violent. Time out.' She points with her clipboard to the stage.

Dragging my axe behind me, I climb up to the stage and sit down with everyone else who's gone 'too far'.

My chin in my hands, I watch the brawl, my eyes always on Hoshi. She moves like she's dancing, constantly darting from person to person. Jake plunges towards her, but she ducks under his arm and pokes him on the bum with her sword. He spins round, but she's already off fighting Betty, who soon discovers wood is stronger than card. When her sword tears in two, she starts using her hands like a ninja, karate-chopping Hoshi's arm.

Next to me, a laugh bursts out of Bus Kelly. When she sees me looking, she covers her mouth. 'What's so funny?' I say.

'She is.' She nods at Hoshi, who now has one hand behind her back like she's fencing. She's waving her sword in tiny circles.

'And she knows it,' I say.

'*Definitely.*'

'Yeah?' I look at her properly. 'Why d'you say that?'

'She *loves* attention.'

'Very observant, Bus Kelly!' I hold up my hand for a high five.

'Thanks!' She slaps her little hand against mine.

'Ew,' I say. 'Sticky!'

'Strawberry Laces,' she says, pulling a handful of sweets out of her pocket. 'Want one?'

'Yeah. Go on.'

She detangles a lace and passes it to me. As I nibble at the lace, I watch the fight. Jake is creeping up on Hoshi. Suddenly he grabs her round the waist and lifts her off the ground. She screams and clutches at his hands, then Jake's face is buried in her neck, close to her ear, like he's whispering something to her.

I feel panic rising inside me. Suddenly I'm sick of

waiting to do something. I need to get a message to her, right now, let her know what it feels like to have something taken away from you. I turn to Kelly. 'Will you do me a favour?' I ask.

'What?' She's dangling a lace over her mouth.

'Take one of the new girl's shoes,' I say, pointing at Hoshi's clumpy shoes that are lined up at the side of the studio, 'and put it somewhere funny.'

She stares at me. 'Where should I put it?'

I sigh. 'The roof of the gym . . . down the toilet . . . I don't know. Use your imagination!'

'Why?'

'Just for a laugh,' I say. 'Go on!'

'Do I have to?' she asks. I stare at her and nod. Slowly, she gets to her feet and, after checking no one's looking, heads down the stairs towards the pile of shoes.

I watch her go, her eyes darting from side to side. Kelly gives me one final glance, then reaches for Hoshi's shoe.

That's when I see her hand is trembling.

'Kelly!' I hiss, and she spins round, dropping the

shoe. I force myself to smile. 'What're you doing? I was joking!'

She grins, relieved, and comes running back up the stairs. 'You're crazy!' she says, sitting down next to me.

'Something like that,' I mutter.

Kelly wriggles a bit closer to me. 'I was going to put it in with Mr Gill's snake,' she says. 'Right in the tank.'

'Yeah?' I say, and I laugh. 'That would have been pretty funny, Kelly.' Then we watch the rest of the fight together, Kelly giving me an ongoing commentary while I work my way through her tangled ball of strawberry laces.

After rehearsal, I persuade Kat to walk part of the way home with me. It's dark and cold, but the rehearsal gives us so much to talk about we hardly notice the wind stinging our faces.

'Who am I?' asks Kat, crouching low in front of me, one leg stretched to the side, arms wide.

'Mr Simms?' I say. At the end of our rehearsal, Ms Kapoor and Mr Simms demonstrated rehearsed stage combat. Mr Simms announced that he needed to change so he could 'move fluidly', then reappeared wearing a pair of silky, clinging trousers: Tai-Chi pants, apparently.

'Who am I now?' She throws her bag at my feet and does a forward roll then leaps up and balances like a stork.

'That would have to be Mr Simms again.' I laugh. 'Oh my God, Kat, you were *that* close to dog poo.'

'Leaves!'

'Poo.'

She waves her hands in front of my face. 'Yield and overcome, Pearl. Bend and be straight!'

'What does that even mean?'

'I don't know,' she says, picking up her bag. 'Even Ms Kapoor was embarrassed when he said it!'

We carry on down the street and I pick a leaf out of her hair. 'Did you see his V.P.L.?'

'He didn't have one.'

'Exactly! They were very clingy trousers . . . Bit suspicious.'

'Shut up!' laughs Kat, hitting me on the shoulder. We've got to the underpass that runs under the dual carriageway. 'Got to go.' Kat's checking her phone. 'Mum's making raclette tonight. My favourite.' I don't know what raclette is, but it sounds good. Like she can read my mind, she says, 'I'd invite you over, but my sister's back from uni. Bit of a family thing.'

'It's alright. Mum's expecting me.'

'I don't think you should walk that way,' she says, glancing at the underpass. Traffic streams endlessly along the road next to us. 'Aren't you scared?'

I laugh. 'No!'

'Text me when you get in.'

'Alright, loser.' I walk down the slope.

'Hey,' Kat calls after me. 'Hoshi's OK, isn't she? She'll be a good Juliet.'

'We'll see!' I shout over my shoulder, then I plunge into the gloom of the underpass, stamping through puddles, the traffic thundering over me.

TEN

I let myself in the house and stand just inside the back door. 'Alfie?' I call out. Then I hear laughter.

I find Mum and Alfie sitting on the sofa in the living room. Ozzie is sprawled across Mum's lap and Alfie's bare feet are buried deep in Ozzie's black and white hair. Mum looks up from *EastEnders* and smiles with her eyes half closed. I know without looking that a bottle of wine will be sitting on the coffee table. 'Hello, love,' she says. 'Come and watch telly.'

'I'm going to check on my fish.'

Mum and Alfie glance at each other and Mum laughs. 'Don't worry,' she says. 'They're not going anywhere. Sit down.'

'OK.' I drop my bag on the floor and slump on the

beanbag. My hands are freezing so I shove them between my knees. Ozzie lifts up her head and fixes me with her ice-blue eyes before flopping back down. 'Hello, Oz,' I say. Mum sips her drink and strokes Ozzie's ear. 'What's for dinner?'

'Spaghetti bolognaise . . . crispy duck and pancakes . . . coq au vin!' says Mum. 'Whatever you're making, love.'

Alfie smiles.

'We haven't got any food,' I say.

'*We haven't got any food,*' says Alfie, copying me.

'Shut up,' says Mum. I'm not sure who she's talking to.

'Or milk . . . or shampoo . . . or −'

'Guess what?' Mum stares at me and Ozzie lifts up her big fluffy head and joins in. 'I've been at work all day, for *ten* hours. So *stop* moaning.'

Suddenly, I'm starving. 'It's alright for you. I bet you ate at the farm.' Mum takes another sip of her wine then bangs the glass down on the coffee table. I force myself to drop the subject. 'Hey, Mum,' I say.

'We're doing a musical of *Romeo and Juliet* at school, and I'm in it.'

'Yeah?' she says. 'I read that at school: "Parting is such sweet sorrow" . . . That's it, isn't it?'

'"That I shall say good night till it be morrow."' I know nearly all of Juliet's lines. Actually, I know most of the play. When I found out we were doing *Romeo and Juliet*, I took a copy from Ms Higginson's cupboard (along with a Terry's Chocolate Orange and some paracetamol) and started reading it every night.

'Who are you?' Mum asks.

'Tybalt.'

Alfie's eyes flick from the screen to me. 'Who?' he says.

'*Tybalt*,' I say.

'I'll come and watch,' says Mum. 'When is it?'

'December. Just before Christmas.'

'We'll both come, won't we, Alfie?'

He reaches for a cup of coffee and takes a sip. 'No,' he says.

'Ignore him,' she says. 'He's in a mood because he drove his bike into the river. We had to use the tractor to pull it out.' Mum laughs and Ozzie jiggles up and down. 'He got his Abercrombie shirt all muddy!'

Mum's laugh gets even louder and I smile, but out of the corner of my eye I see Alfie's jaw tensing. 'Tybalt?' he says suddenly. 'Isn't he a man?'

'In the original play. In this version Tybalt is going to be female.'

Alfie smirks at the screen and Mum lights a cigarette and blows the smoke over her shoulder. 'Who's that?' She points at the screen with her fag. 'Is it thingy's brother?'

'That ugly bloke?' says Alfie. 'The one with the beard and the hairy chest? It's Pearl.'

Mum laughs and tuts.

I get off the beanbag. 'Shut up, Alfie,' I say.

In a flash he's on his feet and Ozzie's scrambling to stay on the sofa. Alfie sticks his face close to mine so our foreheads are nearly touching. Everything about him is hard: his eyes, his muscles, his mouth. 'Why did you tell me to shut up?' he says. 'Who's been talking non-stop since they got in?'

I stare back at him, trying to look just as hard.

'Won't you two *ever* stop fighting?' says Mum. She heaves herself off the sofa and picks up her glass and the bottle of wine. 'C'mon, Ozzie. Let's leave them to it.' She walks away, Ozzie following.

A few seconds later, her bedroom door slams shut.

Alfie's standing so close to me I can actually taste his Lynx Africa. Suddenly he jerks his forehead towards me. I yell and duck out of the way, but he's not even close. 'Should've seen your face!' He laughs. Then he flops back on the sofa, arms sprawled above his head, bare toes wriggling. My heart is hammering and I can still feel where his breath touched me. With shaking hands, I get out the key to my room.

I stay in my room for the rest of the evening. I take loads of cool pictures of Oy going crazy for blood worms and I smoke some fags I pinched out of Mum's bag. I see what everyone's doing online, but I don't post anything. Later, I go to the kitchen to look for something to eat. As I walk past the stairs with some leftover pasta, I see a strip of light at the bottom of Mum's door and I hear her TV. I don't know where Alfie is.

I sit on the floor and eat the pasta. It tastes even better than last night. As I eat, I flick through *Romeo and Juliet*, looking for my favourite lines from the play. When Romeo has been sent away from Juliet and he's lonely and unhappy, he says, *I dreamt my lady came and found me dead . . . And breathed such life with kisses on my lips that I revived and was an emperor*. It's like *Sleeping Beauty*, only the roles are swapped round.

I drop the book and look at my humming, bubbling tank. Oy sticks his head out from behind his rock and I speak the lines to him; the words give me shivers on my skin. 'D'you like it, Oy?' I say. He hovers for a moment, like he's listening, then zips into a tangle of weed.

Suddenly I realise how late it is. I find my baby wipes, pull my mirror on my knees and start to take off my make-up, dropping the orange-stained wipes on the floor as I go. Kat says I should use proper facial ones, but they cost too much. I sweep one across my eyes and gradually my black eyebrows and eyelashes disappear, revealing my pale hairs. I hate them.

Soon my face is blank and my skin is tight and stinging. I turn the tank lights off and climb into bed. I pull the duvet over me and clothes and make-up spill to the floor. 'Night, night,' I say to my fish.

I drift off to sleep imagining I'm playing Juliet. I picture my costume, how my hair's done and even the shoes I'm wearing. I see myself standing in the wings, waiting for my cue. Jake's onstage. He stretches out his hand and I step into the lights . . .

ELEVEN

Mum's been busy. Piled next to the sink is a stack of plates and bowls, bubbles still slipping off them. Two bulging bin bags sit by the back door. She's dumped everything in them: milk cartons, empty cereal packets, Gran's marrowfat peas. There's even some crusty plates in there. I guess she didn't even bother trying to wash them.

The kitchen looks much better. Breakfast is a cup of black tea, but I'm not bothered because there's a note on the table: 'Going shopping after work. Text if you want anything. xxxxx'

I get my phone out. I can't ask for too much or she won't get any of it. Five things are about her limit. Tampons, I text, FRijj milkshakes (chocolate), peanut butter, shampoo (any). Just as I'm trying to decide what the last thing should be, Alfie wanders in. He stares round the empty kitchen, blinks, then goes to the sink.

'Mum's going shopping,' I say.

He grunts and scratches his stomach. He looks like a little boy with his pink cheeks and curly hair all stuck up. He reaches for a mug on the draining board. 'Alfie!' I shout, but I'm too late. The whole slippery pile crashes to the floor – knives, forks, plates and glasses all smash on top of each other. In the silence that follows, I watch as a wine glass teeters on the edge of the worktop before toppling over and shattering. I swallow and shake glass off my foot.

Alfie ignores the chaos around him and runs the tap. When the water's cold, he fills the mug and gulps it down. 'She's going to go mental,' I say. 'Alfie, you've got to clear it up!'

'Why?' He puts his mug upside down on the draining board and steps round the mess, stopping in front of me. 'I didn't do it, Pearl. You did.' Then he walks out of the room and jogs upstairs, taking the steps two at a time.

I look around. I can't let Mum come home and find this! Tonight's going to be *good*. She's going shopping! I look at my phone. My bus goes in ten minutes.

I pull out another bin bag and start stuffing broken glass and china inside, putting away the good stuff as I go. Luckily, not too much is broken. I move quickly and soon I've got little cuts on my fingers from splinters of glass, but I don't stop. I throw knives and forks in the drawer then grab the dustpan and brush and sweep up the bits, chucking them in the bag with the rest of the stuff.

I get down on my hands and knees and scan the floor. I find a couple of shards of glass, drop them in the bag then check the time.

I've got three minutes.

I drag the bin bags to the wheelie bin and then I'm running through the farm and down the track, jumping round muddy puddles and manure. I can see the bus going past the top of the hedge. I force my legs to move faster. God, it hurts. Maybe I should quit smoking again. The bus slows and I yell, 'Wait for me!' getting there just as it's pulling away. 'Stop!' I shout, slamming my hands on the door. The bus driver hits the brakes and stares at me. Then he reaches over, presses a button and the door swings open.

I'm panting as I flop down on the back seat, tired before I've even got to school. I throw my head back and feel the vibrations of the engine running through me. Then I laugh. I actually made it! I get out my phone. **Magnums (raspberry)**, I add to the bottom of my shopping list. Then I press 'send'. You never know.

Tiann doesn't get on the bus, but Hoshi does.

The minute she sees I'm alone, she heads in my direction. I notice that today's 'thing' is a tiny star stuck on the middle of her forehead. '*Konnichiwa*,' I say, as she sits down. 'How's your head?'

'Better,' she says, rubbing her white hair. 'So you've been learning Japanese?'

I hold up my phone. 'This goldfish has been teaching

me. Each time I get a word right, he eats some sushi and gets fatter.' I'm doing it because sometimes Hoshi throws Japanese words into conversations and I want to know what she's saying.

'It's a carp,' she says, looking at my phone. 'He's quite skinny.'

'At the moment. You do it. Eventually he explodes.'

'I don't want to see a carp explode.'

'It's a cartoon!'

She laughs. 'Alright. Give it to me.' It takes her two minutes to make the fish pop, but then we're back at the beginning with another tiny fish. I take my phone back.

'Hey,' she says, staring at my hand. 'You're bleeding!'

'I cut it on glass.'

'You've got cuts all over.'

I wipe my hands on my tights then shove them in my blazer pockets. 'All gone,' I say.

'How did you do it?' she asks.

I sigh and the bus swings round a corner. 'Basically my brother's an idiot who's always breaking stuff. He smashed a glass and I had to clear it up.'

'I'd love to have a little brother. I'm an only child.'

'Alfie's not little,' I say, laughing. 'He's in our Sixth Form. Well, he's in one day a week as part of his apprenticeship, but he hardly ever turns up.'

'Well, I wouldn't care if he was older or younger, I'd still like to have a brother.'

'You can have mine. I hate him.' The bus picks up speed and we bounce from side to side. I realise that talking to Hoshi is distracting me and making me forget why I've bothered talking to her in the first place. This happens sometimes: the whole frenemy thing slips from my mind and I can never work out how she's managed to do it. 'Tell me how to say something funny in Japanese,' I say.

'Like what?'

'Your face looks like a carp's butt.' I stare right at her.

Her eyes narrow. 'OK, so that would be, *Hana no youni kirei.*'

I try it out a few times and Hoshi corrects me until I think I've got it right. 'Hoshi,' I say.

'Yes.'

'*Hana no youni kirei!*'

She laughs. 'Perfect.' The bus sways and we grab the seats in front of us. 'Dancing at rehearsals today,' she says. This afternoon, Ms Kapoor is teaching us the dance she's choreographed for the street fight.

'And the trip next Friday,' I say. 'Are you as good at dancing as you are at singing?'

Hoshi shrugs. 'I'm OK.'

'Because you *can* sing.' The way I say this it doesn't sound like a compliment. I watch her closely. 'Did you do shows back in Japan?'

'Not musicals. I used to dance and sing with my friends, and we did karaoke.'

I stare at her. 'So you got that good at singing by doing karaoke?'

'Yep.' She jumps up and presses the buzzer, even though we're five minutes away from school.

'What're you doing?'

'I'm going to Starbucks. You coming?' She raises her eyebrows. 'I thought you *loved* taking mochas into

91

school.' Then she turns and walks down the aisle. 'I'm paying,' she calls over her shoulder.

After a moment's hesitation, I grab my bag, jump up and follow her. I know I shouldn't, but I really do love mochas.

TWELVE

Hoshi buys herself a hot chocolate and me a mocha. As we walk into school, Hoshi licks whipped cream off a wooden twizzler and tells me all about Japanese karaoke bars. 'My favourite is this one where you can sing from a hot tub,' she says. 'Also, they've got a room called "Heaven" and it has crystals under the glass floor. It's expensive, but so cool.'

'You've been there?'

'Oh . . .' She blows on her drink. 'No. Just heard about it. It's famous.' She sips at her hot chocolate, staring straight ahead over the top of her cup.

Over by the Sixth Form block, Jake Flower is hanging out with a couple of friends. We watch as he kicks a ball against a wall. 'You're going to be kissing him,' I say.

'What?' She looks confused.

'When we start rehearsing the party scene,' I say. 'That's when Romeo and Juliet kiss. Looking forward to locking lips with The Flower?'

She laughs. 'Sure. He's nice . . . *kakkoii*. It means "good looking".'

'Yeah?' I sip my drink. 'What do you like about him?' It's like I'm picking at a scab and I can't stop.

'Some people have dumb eyes – like there's just a blank space behind them – but Jake's got kind eyes.'

'What are mine like?' It just pops out. Why do I care what she thinks about my eyes?

'Yours?' She stops walking and looks at me. I make my eyes big and wide. 'You've got tiger eyes.'

I blink. 'That's evil.'

'Depends if you like tigers,' she says. 'I do.' She stares back at me. 'What are mine like?'

'Pips,' I say. 'Small and black.'

Suddenly, Jake's kicking the ball back to his friends and running to catch up with us. 'How are my Juliets doing?' he asks. Presumably this is supposed to make me feel better.

'This Juliet's got to go,' says Hoshi, turning towards the English block. 'See you at rehearsals, Jake. See you later, Pearl.' Her pip eyes flash at me and then she's walking away.

Jake watches her go then turns to me. 'Where are you off to?'

'Art.'

'I'll come with you.'

As we walk through the school, I notice how many people smile at Jake. Not just girls, but boys too, and teachers. Usually people look at me, then their eyes shoot away like they're scared. With Jake by my side, I'm getting curious glances. Even a few smiles.

He holds a door open for me. 'Can I just say,' he says, as I brush past him, 'you're looking pretty awesome this morning, Harris.'

'Yeah?' I glance across at him.

'I like all this.' He ruffles my tangle of black hair.

I laugh. 'Are you after something?'

'Maybe.' He drops his arm over my shoulder and guides me round a group of Year Sevens. 'I could do with a bit of help.'

He leaves his arm there, warm across my back, and I hardly dare to breathe in case he takes it away. 'What do you need help with?' I ask. 'Your dancing? Because I've noticed you do this weird thing with your hands –'

'As if!' He nudges me. 'You're Hoshi's friend, right?'

'Not really,' I say. 'I mean, we hang out together sometimes.' And even though his hand is still resting on my shoulder, the warmth vanishes and I feel an icy sickness in my stomach. I know what's coming.

'So . . . has she got a boyfriend?'

'She wouldn't go out with you!' My voice comes out loud.

'Why not? I'm great! My mum's always saying it . . . and my nan.'

I force myself to laugh. 'Look, I don't know if she's got a boyfriend.'

'Then find out. Have you got my number?' We're outside my art room. He lets go of my shoulder and gets out his phone. We swap numbers, something I've always wanted to happen. 'You're my wingman, Harris,' he says, putting his hand on my shoulder again. 'Find out what I need to know. Don't let me down!' He smiles his amazing smile then turns and walks away, arms swinging, his T-shirt tight across his shoulders.

A few seconds later, I get a text: **Have a good paint . . . and maybe a chat with Hoshi??** 😊 I grip my phone.

Forget her, I want to text back. **She doesn't need you.**

'Care to join us, Pearl?' calls my teacher.

'Coming.' I rest my head against the wall. My throat is tight. But I don't cry. I never cry. **Will do!** I text Jake. **If anyone can break her, it's me! xox**

I press 'send' and walk into art. 'Hi, Miss!' I say, smiling brightly.

THIRTEEN

I get to French late and there's a free seat next to Hoshi. She smiles up at me, but I keep my face blank and walk past her, dropping into a seat at the back of the room. I'm done with befriending the enemy.

Hoshi turns and tries to catch my eye, so I stare straight at her with my tiger eyes and I don't blink until she looks away.

At the end of the lesson, she waits outside the room. 'Pearl, are you OK?' she asks. Students drift past us. 'What's the matter?' In the distance, two teachers laugh hysterically, then a door slams shut. I don't take my eyes off Hoshi. I don't smile and I don't speak.

For the first time since I met her, a look of

uncertainty flashes across her face, just for a second, and I feel a rush of triumph inside me, a glow. I take one step closer, then another. '*You're* the matter,' I say, then I step round her and walk away.

I do it all day, the stares, the silences, the smiles that aren't really smiles. It means I can't hang out with the girls, but Max is off sick so at least I have Tiann to keep me company. At lunchtime we sit behind the English block, and I listen to Tiann talk about Max's mum's fortieth and ignore all the texts the girls send me.

'This feels just like the old days,' says Tiann happily. I stretch my legs out, kicking litter out of the way, shut my eyes and rest my head on the hard bumpy wall. The weak autumn sun shines on my face and I listen as Tiann lights a fag and inhales deeply. 'Do you want one?' she asks.

I nod and stick out my hand. She's right, I think, as I smoke. This feels exactly like the old days.

After school, Tiann and I are killing time in the girls' toilets when Hoshi walks in. I ignore her and carry on doing my make-up. 'Hey, Pearl,' she says, standing by my side.

In the mirror, I see Tiann's eyes flick over Hoshi. 'What do you think?' Tiann says. 'Bit slutty?' She's talking about the bright pink lipstick she's putting on, but she's looking right at Hoshi.

'Just a bit,' I say.

'Have I done something to upset you?' Hoshi says. Tiann laughs and behind us a toilet flushes. A girl appears, sees the three of us, then disappears out of the door. Hoshi's still watching me as though we're the only people in the room. 'Because I'm getting the feeling you're annoyed with me.'

'Give me that lipstick,' I say to Tiann. 'I'm going to try it.' I push past Hoshi and grab the lipstick off Tiann. I put it on. Hoshi stares at me in the mirror.

'Doesn't suit you,' she says.

I put on even more. 'Concealer, Tiann.'

Grinning, she passes me the tube. 'Can you smell something funny?' she asks.

I feel slightly sick when she says this and a

silence falls over us. 'I said, can you smell something, Pearl?'

I shake my head. 'Leave it, Tiann.'

'What?' She looks at me and laughs.

I stare at the concealer in my hands. 'I said, leave it.' Slowly, I look up and meet Hoshi's gaze.

'*Aitai*, Pearl,' she says, with a trace of a smile, then she turns and walks out of the toilets.

Tiann cackles with laughter. 'What a freak!'

'Shut up, Tiann!'

'What's your problem?'

'*Just stop laughing*,' I say. 'What are you even laughing at?'

'*Her!* The Chinese girl.'

'She's Japanese!'

Tiann scowls at me and turns back to the mirror. I get my phone out and put '*atai*' into Google translate. Was that it? Maybe it was '*attai*'? I keep getting 'or' and 'ouch', which doesn't make sense. While Tiann's going on about Max's puppy, I try out different spellings. Finally, a translation site suggests: '*aitai*: miss you'.

Miss you? Is that what she said?

'Pearl!' says Tiann. 'Are you listening? Max is calling the puppy "Tynan" so it's a bit like my name, but different so he won't get us mixed up.'

I put my phone away and look up at Tiann. 'So he's going to have a girlfriend called Tiann and a dog called Tynan?'

'I know! How sweet?'

'Very,' I say. I feel like I need to make up for what I just said to her. 'Give me your hairbrush.' I tip my head upside down and give my hair a bit of body. I look in the mirror. 'What do you think?'

'You look *boss,* girl,' she says.

'Know it,' I say, and I pick up my bag.

'Look.' She grabs me and shows me her phone. 'Max's just sent me a picture of Tynan chewing his pants . . . cute!'

'Not looking,' I say, pushing the phone away. 'Repulsive. Come on. Walk to the drama studio with me.'

'So who's the new girl in the play?'

'Juliet,' I say as we head down the corridor.

'And Jake Flower's Romeo? Lucky cow. She doesn't deserve him. Not with that face.'

'Tiann.' I stop walking. 'Don't say that! This is nothing to do with you.'

She laughs then stops when she sees my face. 'You're not joking?'

'*No.*'

'What's wrong with you?'

I shake my head and stare at the P.E. noticeboard. I don't know what's wrong with me. I need to get rid of Hoshi so I can be Juliet and have Jake all to myself again, but at the same time I hate hearing Tiann say those things. 'The new girl's my problem,' I say. 'I'll sort her out.'

She shrugs and puts her arm through mine. 'I just don't like seeing someone upsetting my mate,' she says. 'It makes me mad. Y'know what I mean?'

I nod. 'I know what you mean.' We start to walk towards the drama studio. 'Come on, show me those pictures of Tynan and the pants.'

FOURTEEN

Half an hour later Hoshi is sprawled at my feet. 'Sorry,' I say. 'Didn't see you there.'

She takes my hand and jumps to her feet. 'No worries,' she says. I look up and see Betty's beady eyes watching me from under her long fringe. I couldn't resist sticking my foot out just then. I did it without thinking, like swatting a fly.

'Capulets back on the left, Montagues to the right,' says Ms Kapoor. We're working through the opening dance and Jake and Hoshi are joining in even though they won't do it in the show. 'Let's try it again and get it tighter.'

As we sing 'Capulet It Go', we step closer together until the two groups meet, and then we do a cross between a fight and a street dance. I guess it's going to look good when we've got it right, but at the moment it's a mess. We're each paired up with a fighting partner, and mine is Betty.

She kicks her leg high in the air and I duck under it. Then I grab her arm and pull it behind her back. 'Hey,' she whispers when our heads are close together. 'I saw what you just did.'

'What?'

'To Hoshi. Why don't you leave her alone?' I tug her arm back a bit harder than I'm supposed to and she spins out fast, bumping into Jake.

'She tripped over my foot,' I say as I block her blows with my arm. Is she hitting me harder than usual?

'No, she didn't.' *Whack, whack!* 'And I've noticed a few other things you've done recently. I know exactly what you're up to even if Hoshi doesn't.' As Betty swings round I see her eyes are narrowed. 'Do you think you're ever going to get bored of being a bully?'

'Will you ever get bored of being a freak?' I snap back.

She laughs. We're coming up to my favourite bit in the dance. I throw a punch at Betty and she swings her head back like I've made contact. She does it really well. *Smack!* goes my hand. *Thwack!* goes her face. Suddenly, I really, *really* want to make contact and stop all the faking. I pull back my arm and aim my fist at her blunt fringe. My hand brushes her hair as it flies past her face.

'Bit close, you nutter,' she says.

The music stops and I stare at my hand, heart pounding. 'An accident,' I say.

Betty blinks. 'An accident?'

'I'm stressed,' I say. My hands are shaking so I cross my arms and try to get my breathing under control. I take a deep breath. Then another.

'Starting positions,' says Ms Kapoor, clapping her hands.

Betty says quietly, 'What's your problem with Hoshi? I mean, except for the whole stealing your part thing.'

I glance at Hoshi. She's standing with Jake. His

hands are resting on her waist. I shake my head. 'There's no problem,' I manage to say. 'You're imagining it.'

'Positions!' shouts Ms Kapoor.

Betty and I fake-fight so well that Miss gets everyone else to watch us. Then she calls it a night after reminding us to bring in our money for next Friday's trip.

I sit with Kat on the floor as we change our shoes and talk about the weekend. I keep an eye on Hoshi and Jake over by the piano. Hoshi is teaching Jake a dance move. It's so simple, but he just can't get it right.

'Come with me to the shop?' Kat asks, giving my foot a kick. 'Pearl?'

'Yeah, OK.'

Hoshi is heading in our direction. 'Hey,' she says. She's out of breath and her cheeks are rosy. 'Wasn't that fun?'

I stare at her, unsmiling. Kat glances at me, then says, 'Were you just teaching Jake to pop?'

'Trying to. It went wrong. I guess we looked totally dumb.'

She laughs and, without thinking, I copy her stupid laugh even though I can feel Kat's eyes on me. '*Totally,*' I say.

'Shut up, Pearl,' says Kat.

'What?' I force myself to smile. 'It's true. Hoshi looked like a dumbass. She said it herself!' Kat sighs and grabs her bag.

'I just wanted to say that we're going to McDonald's,' says Hoshi. 'Me and Jake. Do you two want to get some food with us?'

'No, thanks,' I say. 'We're walking home.'

'I'll come,' says Kat.

I stare at her. 'I thought we were going to the shop.'

'I don't feel like it any more.'

'What about tomorrow?' We're supposed to be meeting up in town. Kat wants to do some early Christmas shopping.

'Ring me,' she says as she walks away.

'Forget it.' I pull my phone out.

Hoshi's still standing over me. 'Are you sure you don't want to come?'

I ignore her and tap away at my phone. 'We're off, Hoshi!' shouts Kat. Hoshi looks at me for a moment longer, then goes to join the others.

Through my hair, I watch as they leave, Jake holding the door open, Betty pulling Bea along by the sleeve of her coat, Hoshi and Kat at the back, their blonde heads almost touching. Soon the studio is empty, just me and Mr Simms. He turns the lights off one by one. 'Haven't you got a home to go to?' he asks.

'I'm going,' I say, sticking my headphones in. Then I turn my music up loud and brush past him.

I walk out of school and across the field, stamping through piles of wet autumn leaves, drizzle hitting my face. My mind is going crazy with the thought of them sitting together in McDonald's, smiling and laughing, while I'm out here on my own in the dark.

I want to scream, but instead I turn my music up loud until it matches the noise in my head. Hoshi's taking everything away from me, and I'm the only one who seems to have noticed.

FIFTEEN

Hoshi's smile is stuck in my head the whole weekend, distracting me, driving me mad, and even when I'm at World of Water I can't stop thinking about her. I didn't ring Kat on Saturday. I knew there was no point.

On Monday, I still can't bring myself to speak to Hoshi, which means I can't hang out with the girls. Somehow, without anyone saying anything, it's clear that I can't have them without her. But I do have Tiann because she's on one of her monthly break-ups with Max. Then Tiann gets back together with Max and suddenly I'm on my own.

I get to lessons late and the minute the teacher says we can go I'm the first out of the door. At lunch and breaktime, I walk out of school and sit on a bench in the park, smoking and listening to music. No one seems to notice I'm leaving school. Mrs P even stops me in the corridor to tell me how pleased she is that I'm staying out of trouble. 'You've not been sent out of any lessons for a month!' she says.

I reek of fags and my hands are icy, but I just grin and say, 'Thanks, Miss!'

'I'm still watching you,' she adds and my smile vanishes the second she walks away.

I keep this up until Friday, the day of the trip.

As I'm walking to the station I imagine sitting on my own on the train, or worse, Miss and Sir making me sit with them. I also think about what Hoshi said. '*Aitai*, Pearl.' Miss you.

That's when I decide to take a quick detour to Asda to buy a peace offering.

'Hey, losers!' I say when I find the girls on the train. 'Move up. I've got doughnuts.' They give me the uncertain look that I've been getting all week, but then Bea wriggles along the seat so I can sit down.

Hoshi isn't with them, which makes what I have to do a bit easier. 'Betty, Kat, mini strawberry doughnut?'

'Pink sprinkles,' says Bea, and she actually licks her lips. 'Go on, then.'

Betty takes one with narrowed eyes, then I hold the box across the aisle to Kat. 'If I eat a doughnut,' she says, 'I'm not saying I'm cool with what you've been doing to Hoshi . . . but I do want to eat one. Badly.'

'Eat it,' I say, sticking the box under her nose, 'and I promise to be nice to her. I've had enough of you all treating me like I'm Satan.'

Kat takes a doughnut and puts the entire thing in her mouth.

'Wow,' says Betty. 'Was that a challenge?' She takes another doughnut out of the box, stacks it on top of the one she's already holding and opens her mouth as wide as it can possibly go.

'No, Betty,' says Ms Kapoor as she walks down the carriage doing a head count. 'Dangerous.'

'I can do three,' says a voice by my shoulder.

Hoshi is standing in the aisle wearing ridiculously

baggy tracksuit bottoms, a Barbie vest and a knitted cardi. Somehow she's twisted her white hair into two horns on each side of her head. 'Speaking of Satan . . .' I say. Three pairs of eyes shoot on to me. 'Joke!' I say. 'C'mon, Hoshi.' I wriggle up closer to Bea. 'Room for a little one.'

She looks at me for a second, in the way that she does, like we're sharing a joke that no one else is in on, then drops into the seat. 'Like I said –' her hand plunges into the box – 'I can do three.' She sticks them in her mouth just as Ms Kapoor walks back down the carriage.

Miss points a finger at me. 'I'm going to confiscate those doughnuts, Pearl, if I see any more silly games.'

'Do you want one, Miss?'

'Yes.' She puts one on each index finger. 'This one's for Mr Simms,' she says, wiggling it around.

'Miss,' I say, 'can we go to Oxford Street when we're in London?'

'No.'

'Just Zara?'

'No, we haven't got time. We'll be going straight to the dance studio.'

'But look at Hoshi.' I point at her baggy pants. 'She *needs* Zara. It would be cruel to say no.'

'Pearl!' says Kat, scowling, but Hoshi is laughing, her mouth stuffed full of doughnut and pink icing.

'You'd all better be on your best behaviour,' says Ms Kapoor. 'If anyone causes any trouble, they'll find themselves out of the show.' No one's fooled by the 'anyone'. We all know who she means.

'Tough talk, Miss.' I smile up at her.

'I mean it.'

'We're not going to cause any trouble,' says Betty. 'We're going to *knit*.' She pulls two knitting needles out of her bag.

'Well, OK,' says Miss, then she carries on down the carriage, nibbling her doughnut.

'Who wants me to knit them some Domo-kun wrist warmers?' Betty asks. She stares at me, as though this is some sort of niceness test.

'I do,' I say. 'I absolutely want you to do that.'

'You've got to wear them.'

'Definitely.' Betty finds a ball of brown wool and her fingers start flying. 'Kat,' I say. 'I notice you've brought your ukulele with you. Please will you teach me a song?' I smile sweetly at her.

'Abba?' she asks. '"Dancing Queen"?'

'Actually,' I say, 'I'd genuinely like to be able to play that.'

'Awesome!' says Bea, eyes wide. 'Pearl's joining our uke band. We're called the Tampongs.'

'No, she's not,' I say. Then I stick out my wrists so Betty can measure them. 'How quickly can you knit those things?'

'I should have them done before we get to London.'

'Oh, great.'

'We'll start with the C chord,' says Kat, passing me her baby guitar.

We fly past towns and fields, and when we stop at Gatwick, I'm wearing one wrist warmer and I can do the chorus of 'Dancing Queen'. We sing it repeatedly as we go through the suburbs of London and I've pretty much nailed it by the time we get to Victoria. An old guy with a harmonica even joined in, but he had to get off at Clapham.

At Victoria, we walk down the platform laughing and singing, and Kat slips her arm through mine. Today I'm going to make myself forget that Jake likes Hoshi, that she's the star of the show while I'm killed off halfway through. The sun's shining, I'm going to be dancing all day and I'm in London with my friends. That box of pink doughnuts was so worth it.

SIXTEEN

We might have walked straight past Pineapple Dance Studios if their famous neon sign wasn't glowing above the door.

As everyone piles in, I hang back, looking up at the tall red brick building with its arched windows. Then, when the street is almost empty, I go into the foyer and take in the polished floor, white walls and pink, swirly letters of the Pineapple logo across the wall. A woman is chatting to the receptionist, bag dropped by her side. Her leg muscles are defined and her waist is slim and brown. I can smell the take-out coffee she's holding in one hand.

This is my dream. Living in London, miles away from home, dancing every day.

'Come on, Pearl.' Mr Simms is holding a door open

and Hoshi is standing with him, waiting for me. I take one last look around, then follow them inside.

After getting changed we go into studio seventy-nine. It's such a cool space, not because it's smart, but because it's scruffy. Huge windows line one wall and sunlight streams in, showing marks on the floor made by real dancers and drifting dust. There's a long barre, white painted brick walls and a mirror that stretches the length of the room. I stare at my reflection and see my smile.

'Relax for a minute,' says Ms Kapoor. 'Kieron should be here soon.'

'Oh no, you don't,' says Betty as I start to peel off the wrist warmer. 'You said you'd wear it all day.'

'But it's itchy,' I say. 'Plus, it's ruining my look.' Every time I glance in the mirror I see the ugly brown wrist warmer clashing with my baggy vest and leggings.

'Keep it on. It's your punishment for being such a bitch to Hoshi all week.'

I see Hoshi standing at the back with Jake, sharing some water.

'I've had my punishment,' I say. I pull off the wrist warmer and throw it down with my stuff.

'Stop it,' says Betty.

'What?'

'You're watching her again, and you've got that look on your face.' She scowls to show me what she means.

I force myself to smile. 'See,' I say. 'Not bothered.'

Just then, the door opens and a man walks in. 'Here's my crew!' he says, arms spread wide.

'Kieron!' says Ms Kapoor. If I'm honest, I'm a bit disappointed. He doesn't look like a dance teacher. He looks more like a dad wearing his son's Adidas tracksuit.

'Kieron?' he asks, dropping his arm round Miss's waist. 'I'm Kai now . . . Good to see you've still got those snake hips, Kunnali.'

'*Ms Kapoor*,' she says.

Kai laughs and walks to the front of the studio. 'Who's ready to get *funkdafied*?' he asks. Everyone stares at their feet. 'Get into three lines,' he says, clapping his hands. Then he points a remote at the ceiling and music blasts into the room. 'Let's warm up!' As we're still arranging ourselves, Kai starts to dance. Wow . . . Now he doesn't look like a dad!

'Let's see your dougies!' he calls out.

'What's he talking about?' Betty hisses at me. 'I don't understand his words!'

But Kai is such a good teacher it doesn't matter who knows what a dougie is, because soon we're all doing them, even Betty, again and again and again. Then we're swag walking, kick crossing and doing the nae nae. He works us hard for ten minutes then tells us to take a break.

'If that was the warm-up,' says Betty, gulping down water, 'how am I going to survive the actual dance?'

'Well, I love it,' says Kat. 'I feel totally funkdafied . . . and sweaty. Have I got patches?' She examines each armpit.

'Yep,' says Bea. 'You're basically one big patch.'

'Gross.' She uses a scarf to wipe her face.

Bea looks horrified. 'That's mine!'

'Really? I thought it was a towel.' She shrugs and wipes down her arms. 'I might as well carry on now.'

In the end, we all use Bea's scarf. 'It's like we're sweat

sisters,' says Betty as she finds a dry bit to dab at her neck. Bea snatches it off her.

'Back in positions,' says Kai. 'This is going to be the dance that the whole company does in the lead up to –' he swings round and points at Jake and Hoshi – 'your *steamy* kiss!'

Ms Kapoor pulls a face. 'It's just a kiss,' she says. 'No steam required.'

'After learning my routine, it's going to be *hot*.' A few students laugh, but I stare straight ahead, trying not to lose the amazing buzz I've got from the dancing.

'Well . . .' says Miss. 'Maybe warm.'

'*Hot*,' insists Kai, then he explains the dance, moving round the room, rearranging us slightly. I'm in the centre, just behind Hoshi and Jake. 'This is the party scene, so the dance is going to be high-energy hip hop and full of saucy moves.' Ms Kapoor's eyes widen. 'Are we ready?' He dashes back to the front of the class. 'Let's start with the chicken noodle soup dance.'

It turns out I love doing the chicken noodle, but the hip moves are hard so I have to concentrate. As I follow

Kai's routine, repeating each move again and again, I forget Jake and Hoshi and I find myself in the moment, my body and mind light and free. Then Kai says we're ready to 'jam it out' and we do everything we've learnt with minimal instructions.

'You,' Kai shouts, pointing at me. 'Girl with all the hair and legs. Loving your style.' I don't miss a beat as we drop down low then pop straight up again. 'And Juliet.' Kai nods. 'Nice. You've had training.'

My eyes flick to Hoshi. Kai's words have thrown her and she turns in the wrong direction. She corrects herself and she's back in the routine, but now I can't take my eyes off her and soon I notice something: even though she knows every move and her timing is perfect, she keeps making mistakes, and they're such basic mistakes it just doesn't make sense.

'Concentrate, big hair!' Kai shouts. I force myself to look straight ahead, but then, out of the corner of my eye, I see that Hoshi is watching me in the mirror, just like I was watching her. She winks, then we're spinning away from each other to finish the dance.

Next, Miss explains that they've built pauses into the dance for me, Hoshi and Jake to say our lines. When Tybalt sees Romeo at the party, he's furious and tries to get him chucked out, but Romeo stays and goes on to kiss Juliet. We run through the dance slowly, but this time the three of us speak as well. We do this a couple more times, each time stopping just before the kiss.

'It works.' Ms Kapoor smiles and nods her head. 'Now let's try it with the music and we'll finish with the kiss.'

I feel a bit sick. I ate too many doughnuts on the train, but then the music starts and I have to slide to the left with everyone else, my arms crossing in front of my face.

At the first pause, I say, '"Villain,"' staring in Romeo's direction. '"I'll not endure him!"'

'Good,' Ms Kapoor calls over the music. 'Nice hatred, Pearl.'

A few seconds later, Romeo and Juliet notice each other and start to move closer. They meet, Jake takes Hoshi's hand and I hiss, '"It makes my flesh tremble",' into the silence. Music comes back on, but quieter now, and we continue with the dance while Hoshi and Jake say their lines. I speak Juliet's lines too, silently in my head, all the time stepping back with the rest of the company – Miss doesn't want anyone to distract from 'her stars'.

'"Move not",' says Jake, pulling Hoshi closer, '"while my prayer's effect I take."' There's a break in the music – a skipped heartbeat – and we freeze. Hoshi shuts her eyes and Jake kisses her on the lips. The room is silent. I can feel my heart thudding and I can feel the kiss that has been stolen from me. I shut my eyes too. I just can't watch.

The heavy bass kicks back in and we all step back into the dance, but I can't escape the image – in front of me and reflected in the wall-to-ceiling mirrors – of Hoshi and Jake still wrapped in each other's arms.

The music stops and all around me people flop down or grab water, but Jake and Hoshi stand there, chests touching, faces millimetres apart.

'I've got goosebumps!' says Ms Kapoor, clasping her hands together.

SEVENTEEN

'Stay together,' says Mr Simms, trying to count our heads. It's rush hour at Victoria station and, all around us, commuters push past, coffees held high, phones pressed to their ears. They look pretty irritated to find a big group of teenagers blocking their path, especially as most of the teenagers are doing the chicken noodle.

'I never thought I'd say this, guys,' says Ms Kapoor, 'but *please* stop dancing.'

'We can't, Miss!' says Betty, then she starts to do the chicken noodle around her. 'Kai's made us too funky!'

Ms Kapoor snatches Betty's cupcake hat off her head. 'I'm warning you, Betty Plum. *Stop dancing.*'

Betty laughs crazily and dances away.

'That girl drank too much Mountain Dew,' says Kat.

After the rehearsal we discovered a vending machine in the foyer that sold loads of sweets and drinks from America. Before the teachers noticed, we'd raided it and now we're on serious sugar highs.

'I can see it,' says Bea, drifting away from the group. Kat pulls her back. 'What?'

'Krispy Kreme Doughnuts!'

'I never want to see another doughnut again in my life,' says Kat. 'Hey.' She nudges me. 'Why are you so quiet?'

'Tired,' I say. My muscles are aching, but in a good way. What I'm tired of is the jealous ache in my chest that came back the moment I saw Hoshi and Jake kiss. I've tried to push the feeling away but I can't seem to escape from it. It was there on the tube when they swayed against each other, and I'm feeling it right now, because I've just seen Jake look in Hoshi's direction.

'Platform fourteen!' shouts Ms Kapoor. 'This way. Stick together.'

Hoshi appears by my side. 'Are there toilets on the train?' she asks. 'I've drunk too much Hawaiian Punch.'

She looks so happy, smiling up at me, that I just have

to say something to bring her down. 'No. They're kept locked in case terrorists leave bombs in them.'

'Oh, God,' she says, eyes wide. 'But I'm desperate!'

My mind starts ticking. 'There's the toilet,' I say, pointing towards a row of turnstiles, 'but Miss won't let you go.'

'I *have* to.' Her face lights up. 'I'll run. They won't even notice I'm gone. Which platform does the train go from?'

And that's when Hoshi hands it to me: the moment I've been waiting so patiently for. 'Platform thirteen,' I say with a smile and immediately I feel lighter, better.

She dashes towards the turnstiles. 'Cover for me!' she calls over her shoulder. I watch as she weaves between people and suitcases, then fumbles for a coin before disappearing into the toilets.

I laugh, amazed at what has just happened. My heart speeds up. Leaving the group in central London, deliberately disobeying the teachers. That's not good. It's probably not enough to get Hoshi thrown off the show, but who knows? . . . Maybe it is!

'Keep up, Pearl!' shouts Mr Simms.

'Coming!' I run forward and link arms with Kat and Betty. 'Rock yo' hips,' I say, bumping into them.

'Shoulder lean,' says Betty, adding a new move.

'Come here, Bea,' says Kat, pulling Bea on to the end of the line. We follow our teachers, doing our stupid dance and getting evils from all the boring people in suits.

'My butt is so funkdafied!' yells Bea, which is suddenly the funniest thing she could possibly say and we all collapse laughing.

'Girls,' shouts Ms Kapoor. 'Stop showing off.' This only makes the four of us laugh even harder and suddenly I'm happier than I have been for days.

By the time we get to our platform the train is already crammed with passengers.

'This is a nightmare,' says Mr Simms as we walk past carriage after carriage, each one as full as the one before. 'What shall we do?'

'We just need to get on,' says Ms Kapoor, glancing at

her phone. 'It goes in a couple of minutes. They're a sensible bunch.' As she says this, she glances at me. 'Listen,' she says, raising her voice. 'We can't sit near each other. We can't even get in the same carriage. So I want you all to get into small groups and *stick together*. You've got my mobile number, and I've got yours, so check for messages. We'll come and find you once we're on our way.'

All along the train, doors start closing. 'What are you waiting for?' asks Mr Simms.

'Come on.' I drag Kat back down the platform. 'I saw a seat.'

'*A* seat? What good's that?' she says. Betty and Bea follow us.

'Let's just get away from the teachers,' I say. We jump into the next carriage and stand right by the door. We can't get any further on to the train.

'This is exactly what I want after all that dancing,' says Betty, flopping back against the wall. 'A nice bit of standing.'

'Girls,' says Bea, peering out of the door. 'Is that *Hoshi*?'

Betty and Kat look over her shoulder. On the opposite platform is another train and sitting by the window, all on her own, is Hoshi. She's frowning and staring at her phone. 'It is Hoshi!' yells Kat, banging on the glass. 'I bet she's trying to ring us. *Hoshi!*'

'She can't hear you,' I say.

Betty's got her phone out. 'There's no reception!'

'There's nothing we can do,' I say, leaning against the luggage rack. 'Our train is about to go.' As one, they turn and stare at me. '*What?*'

'Why are you smiling?' says Kat.

'Am I?' I'm laughing now, I just can't help it. 'It's funny. She's got on the wrong train . . . for some reason.'

'Oh my God,' says Bea. 'It was *you*. You told her to get on that train.'

'I didn't!' But they just know me too well, and I can't get rid of my smile.

'Stop it!' says Bea, stepping closer to me, her face pale. 'This isn't funny, Pearl. Stop smiling!' Her voice is furious. 'These *funny* things you do hurt. I can still remember exactly what it feels like.'

A silence has fallen over the carriage and people are turning round to stare. Now my smile has gone.

'You act like you've changed,' she says, pointing a finger in my face, 'but you haven't. That stuff you did to me in Year Nine – the texts, the names, the things written on my locker, *the black eye* – you did it all that because you were jealous and wanted what I had. Well, *nothing's* changed, has it? Hoshi's got something you want and you can't stand it!'

I try to speak, but my throat has gone dry. Kat and Betty look just as angry as Bea. She takes a step closer to me. 'You get Hoshi off that train, Pearl . . .'

'Or what?' I manage to say.

'Or *we* are over,' she says. Kat and Betty stare at me in silence and I know she's speaking for all of them.

I look at Bea, this girl who I've known for so many years, who's shaking at the memory of things I said and did to her.

'I'm sorry,' I say. And I really am.

Then I turn round, hit the button and the door hisses

open. I jump off the train and run across the empty platform. I have to get Hoshi off that train!

A guard is standing next to Hoshi's train, whistle in her mouth, arm raised. I hammer on the window until Hoshi looks up. 'Get off!' I shout. 'You're on the wrong train!'

She frowns and stares at me.

'Hoshi!' I beg. 'Just get off the train!'

She jumps to her feet. 'You!' the guard yells at me. 'Move away from the train.'

I shake my head. 'My friend's getting off!'

'Too bad,' she says. 'Stand back. This train is departing!'

I ignore her and run to the door. I press my finger down on the button and keep it there. *Come on, come on!* I see Hoshi pushing her way through the carriage. Behind me the last doors shut on our train.

'Step back, young lady.' The guard marches towards me just as the doors slide open and Hoshi tumbles out.

'Quick,' I say, grabbing her wrist. We spin round, but our train is already moving along the platform, sliding away from us. I run towards it, dragging Hoshi behind me. Bea, Kat and Betty are still standing by the door, their hands pressed against the glass, eyes wide open. 'You should have kept the door open!' I yell. 'I got her!' But they can't hear me and the train picks up speed and snakes out of the station.

I let go of Hoshi's wrist and sink to the dusty ground. Hoshi stares after the disappearing train. 'It was never platform thirteen, was it?' she says.

I press my fingers into my eyes. My head is throbbing. 'No.' I look up. Both trains have gone and the platform is strangely quiet. A pigeon lands next to me and starts pecking at a bit of croissant. It watches me with a yellow eye.

Hoshi turns to face me, strands of her bleached hair sticking out of her horns. Her eyes are wide. 'Looks like we're stranded,' she says with a smile.

EIGHTEEN

Ten minutes later, we're sitting on a bench furiously texting. **Yo miss am on train with hoshi but can't see you!! I think we're carriage 6 or it might be 3 ☺ x pearl**

Hoshi sends a similar message to Miss while I text Kat. **Me and hoshi will get next train SAY WE ARE ON TRAIN!!! Ps thanks for holding it up for us dumbass (pass this message on to bea and betty)**

We're in the quietest bit of the station we could find, opposite a pasty shop. I stare at the rows of greasy golden pasties until I get a reply. **This is KARMA. Will try to cover for you. Say hi to Hoshi. xox Kat ps you're the dumbass obvs**

After a moment, I text back: **I know.** Then I go back

to staring at the pasties. How could I have made such a mess of things?

'Listen to this,' says Hoshi. 'Ms Kapoor says she can't move up or down the train because it's too crowded and that we should make sure we find her when we get off.'

I look up at her. 'So we might actually get away with this? The next train goes in half an hour!'

'There's only one problem.'

'What?'

'No tickets.'

She's right. We were on a group ticket and Ms Kapoor had them all. 'We'll buy one,' I say, pulling out my wallet.

Hoshi turns to face me, crossing her legs on the bench. She unzips her panda purse and shakes the contents on to my rucksack. 'Oh,' she says. 'I've got two pounds.'

I push my fingers into the corners of my wallet and drop a few coins next to hers. 'I haven't even got that!' I say with a groan.

'Don't look so worried.'

'I can't help it. Unlike you, I'm on, like, my last, *last* chance at school!'

'Why? What've you done?'

'Pretty much everything.'

Hoshi smiles. 'Yeah?'

'*Yeah,*' I say. 'So we can't ring Ms Kapoor or I'll definitely be thrown off the show.' My shoulders slump. 'I could even get excluded.'

'We just need some money.' Hoshi pulls her cardigan tight around her. Even though it's warm for autumn, a freezing wind is blowing through the station.

I look up as two police officers stroll round the corner. They're wearing chunky black vests with guns slung across their shoulders. 'Well, *obviously*,' I whisper.

'Hello, girls,' says the police woman, her radio buzzing. 'What are you two up to?'

'Going to Covent Garden,' says Hoshi, scooping all the coins into her purse and jumping to her feet. 'Come on, Ruby.' I sit on the bench, blinking up at her. '*Ruby.*' Hoshi's eyes go wide. 'Mum's waiting for us at Belgo. We're going to be late for our *moules.*'

The police officers glance at each other.

136

I stand up and Hoshi pulls me towards an exit. 'I love *moules*!' I shout over my shoulder.

We run down some steps into the Underground. 'So where *are* we going?' I say.

'Like I said, Covent Garden.'

'Hoshi,' I stop walking and a flood of people stream past us, 'we haven't even got enough money to buy two tube tickets!'

'We're not buying tickets,' she says, then she plunges forward into the crowd. I catch up with her by the ticket barriers. Hoshi's stopped a woman with a back pack. 'Excuse me,' she says. 'Have you finished with your travel card?'

'Sure,' says the lady, passing Hoshi her ticket.

Hoshi turns round and grins at me. 'Simples,' she says. 'Only ask people with tickets in their hands. No one's going to give us their Oyster card. Oh, and go for tourists and make sure the tube staff don't see you.'

I stare at her. For someone who couldn't work out that I sent her to the wrong platform, she seems to know a lot about the London Underground. 'What are we actually going to do when we get there?' I say, but Hoshi has already turned round and is approaching an elderly Japanese couple. I watch as she chats away in Japanese, her face tilted to one side, all cute and innocent. I've seen her do this so many times at school.

'Excuse me,' I say to a man passing by. He looks up, frowning, one arm tightening on the strap of his bag. 'Have you finished with your ticket?'

'Sorry,' he says. 'Still need it.' He pushes past me.

Hoshi appears at my side. 'Got one,' she says, handing it to me. 'Got two actually, and some Marukawa gum.' She holds out a wrapped sweet. 'Want one?'

I follow Hoshi through the ticket barrier and unwrap my chewing gum on the escalator. Hoshi turns round so she's going down backwards. 'They're squidgy, aren't they?' She chews and shuts her eyes for a moment. Then pops them back open. 'Now you know what Japan tastes like.'

'Strawberry?'

'Yep.'

'What are we doing?' I can't believe we're heading

down into the Underground, actually getting further away from home. Warm air blows up the escalator. 'How can we get money at Covent Garden? I need to get back.'

'You'll see,' she says.

'Just tell me.'

'Are your parents expecting you?'

'*Parent*. My mum. No, not on a Friday night.' Hoshi steps off the escalator and I follow. 'I did have a curfew,' I say, 'but she gave up on it ages ago.'

'So, what's the rush? We'll get some money then go back.' Without even looking at the list of stations, she takes the passage towards the Victoria line. 'Trust me!' she calls over her shoulder.

I watch her go. Maybe I could go back into the station and try to sneak on to the train. Hide in the toilets or something. But if I got caught I'd be in even more trouble. Plus, I can't shake the feeling that whatever Hoshi is up to, I have to go along with it, see this thing that I started through to the end.

'Wait for me!' I shout, then I push against the crowd of people towards her.

NINETEEN

When we come out at Covent Garden it's nearly dark. We walk towards the main plaza, past Monsoon, a juggler and at least three human statues. Lights are strung across the road and shop windows are full of fake presents, snowflakes and glittery dresses. A group of people wearing Santa hats and Shelter T-shirts are shaking buckets of coins.

I check my phone. Our train will be getting in soon. I've had loads of texts. The last one was from Betty: **Miss just found us. I said you and Hoshi had gone looking for a toilet 'with paper' lols. She didn't seem bothered. Looks like you're gonna get away with it. Amazeballs!!!**

But I can't relax, not until I know they're off the

train and everyone is heading home. I drop my phone in my bag. 'What are you looking for?' I ask.

Her eyes flick up and down each road. 'The right spot.'

'For what?' I'm starting to get hungry, and my feet are killing me from all the dancing.

'This way.' She walks towards a theatre tucked away down a side street, stopping outside a crowded pub. Post-work drinkers spill out on to the street, laughing and blowing smoke from their fags into the air. Hoshi walks up to a man. 'Excuse me,' she says. 'Can I borrow your hat?'

Instinctively, his hand goes to the black cap he's wearing. 'Sorry?' He laughs, confused.

'Your hat. I need it. Just for five minutes. I promise to give it back.'

The man frowns, but then Hoshi does her special smile and the woman next to him squeezes his arm. 'Don't be so mean,' she says. 'Let her have it!'

With a sigh, the man hands it over. It has 'SECRET AGENT' written across the front.

Hoshi does a quick bow. '*Arigatou,*' she says, then she

passes it to me, pulls off her cardi and stuffs it in her bag. Standing in the middle of the wide pavement, she faces the pub. 'Who wants to see a show?' she shouts out.

What? Quickly I step back as Hoshi spins round and calls to the tourists walking past, 'Where are you going? The show's about to start! Don't be shy. Gather round.' She beckons people closer and, amazingly, they start to form a semi-circle round her. 'I'm going to sing for you!' she announces.

'What's she doing?' says a girl standing behind me, and her boyfriend laughs. Hoshi just ignores all the stares and giggles, lifts her chin and waits until everyone falls quiet. I want to disappear, but I'm trapped, surrounded by people on all sides.

Suddenly Hoshi's voice rises above the traffic and distant sirens, strong and perfectly clear, stopping the chatter from the pub and making people stare. She's singing her solo from the show, 'What's in a Name?', a slow and beautiful song and the only one that Mr Simms actually wrote. She puts her hands behind her back and closes her eyes, effortlessly hitting the high notes. All around me people smile and I know that her voice is getting inside them, working its magic.

As she sings, Hoshi turns slowly. When she sees me, she raises her eyebrows and nods. Then I get what she wants me to do. I walk around the circle, cap stretched out, and coins start to fall inside.

Hoshi finishes the song to loud applause. She smiles sweetly and I keep shaking the hat under people's noses. I may not want to be doing this, but if people stood there listening to Hoshi sing they should at least pay up. 'Want to see us do a dance?' she asks the crowd. I freeze at the word 'us', but all around people are clapping and, even though the hat is getting heavy, I know we haven't got enough money yet. 'Come on, Pearl,' she says.

I shake my head. 'No way,' I mutter. Performing in a theatre is one thing, but here on the street?

'Oh, go on, Pearl,' says a lady holding her daughter's hand, and then everyone joins in, patting me on my back and telling me to get up there and help my friend out.

I look at Hoshi and sigh. 'What?' she says, laughing.

'This is all your fault.' I pull off my hoodie and drop it on the floor next to the cap.

Everyone is delighted that I've been bullied into dancing and their claps and shouts of 'Go, Pearl!' only encourage more people to stop and see what's going on.

'We only learnt this dance today,' says Hoshi, 'and we're going to need you to help out.' She starts the clapping, getting the rhythm right. 'Come on,' she shouts to the people outside the pub. 'Put those drinks down and make some noise!' Soon most people are joining in. 'Ready, Pearl?' She grins at me.

'No,' I say, feeling my cheeks burn.

'Great,' she says. 'Then let's go.'

We start Kai's routine to whoops and cheers and almost immediately I'm enjoying myself. I know I'm good at dancing and I can't help loving the attention.

Halfway through the dance, Hoshi speeds up. It's like she can't hold back any more and I finally see what she was trying to hide at the dance studio.

Hoshi's not OK at dancing. She's *amazing*.

Every move she makes is lightning fast and utterly

144

laid back. After a quick chicken noodle soup that is ten times better than Kai's, she drops down and starts to breakdance.

The crowd roars their approval and this is when I stop dancing, step back and find myself watching Hoshi along with everyone else. Her bleached blonde hair shines in the darkness and as her moves get more acrobatic I see just how strong she is. She does a series of monkey flips across the pavement before rolling back on her shoulders and flipping effortlessly back to her feet.

As I watch her, this tiny figure surrounded by adoring strangers, I realise the prickle of irritation isn't there. In fact, I'm looking at Hoshi and thinking, *That's my friend you're all gazing at . . .*

I'm so distracted by her dancing that I almost forget the hat. I grab it off the ground and take it round the audience. This time, loads of coins go in and even some notes. I glance back at Hoshi, wondering how long she can keep this up. She grins at me, but then I see her frown and glance over my shoulder. Someone behind me is shouting, 'Hoshi! Hoshi!' again and again.

145

I turn round. Two Japanese girls are jumping up and down. 'Hoshi!' they shout. One of the girls has her phone out and is filming Hoshi dance.

Hoshi does a final boomerang flip. 'That's it,' she says, grabbing our bags off the floor. 'Show's over.'

But no one's going anywhere – they all applaud and shout for more. Hoshi puts her hands together and bows quickly, turning round the circle, then she beckons me to follow her through the crowd. As we pass by the two girls, one of them says something to Hoshi in Japanese. She just shakes her head and steps round her.

Then, through a gap in the crowd, I see a policeman walking towards us.

'Time to go!' I say to Hoshi, grabbing her arm. We push our way out of the group. When I look back, the policeman is jogging in our direction. 'Go . . . go!' I shout to Hoshi, shoving her ahead of me.

We run past the theatre and down a narrow road, the policeman following. As we dash across a junction, I come so close to a taxi that I have to slam my hand on its bonnet. A horn blares and I catch a glimpse of the driver's furious face before Hoshi pulls me back on to the pavement and we're heading down an even narrower road that twists and turns. Eventually we find our way blocked by a huge road. Beyond the road is the Thames.

We cross between cars, running to make it to the other side. 'Has he gone?' I ask, gasping for breath.

Hoshi peers behind us. 'Definitely gone,' she says. Then we start laughing and we don't stop until we've crossed a bridge and are walking on the other side of the river, shoulders heaving, chests burning.

That's when I look down at my hand. 'Oh no, Hoshi,' I say, holding up the cap. 'Look what we stole!'

Her eyes go wide. 'Now we're fugitives!'

TWENTY

We decide to walk back to Victoria along the Embankment because Hoshi says the Underground is 'too dangerous for criminals'. Personally, I think the police will have bigger things to worry about on a Friday night than two girls nicking a cap, but it's kind of cool wandering along by the river, passing Big Ben and the London Eye.

A text from Kat tells us that they're at the station, but it's so crowded she doesn't think the teachers will notice we're missing. Quickly, I send Ms Kapoor a text: **Can't see you — me and hoshi have gone home. Have a good weekend! x pearl**

A minute later, I get a reply: **Glad you got back safely. See you on Monday! x Miss.** 'We actually did it,' I say, staring at my phone. Then I feel a rush of excitement. 'It's Friday night, and we are out *in London*.'

'Awesome, right?' Hoshi shuts her eyes and breathes in deeply. 'I love the smell of cities. It reminds me of Tokyo.' She's taken out her hair-horns and her hair is sticking out underneath the stolen cap. 'Except the buildings. In Tokyo they are twice as high and covered in lights. I wish you could see them.'

We walk beside the dark glittering river, past girls shivering in tiny dresses and tourists looking for places to eat. 'So,' I say, giving her a nudge, 'you did some OK dancing back there.'

She jumps up on a wall and walks along it doing some pops and locks. 'Thanks,' she says. Then she laughs. 'I guess I didn't want to show off at the dance studio.'

'And what were those girls saying to you?'

She shrugs. 'Just wanted to know if I was Japanese.' Hoshi spins round, arms spread wide like a ballerina.

'How come they knew your name?'

'They didn't.'

I laugh. She's not getting away with this. 'Yes, they did. I heard them say "Hoshi".'

'That's because *hoshi* means "star". Mum gave me a non-traditional name. It's like someone being called "Sky" or "Blossom" over here. Those girls were just trying to get my attention because I was the one dancing.' She jumps over a gap in the wall and I run to catch up with her. 'Watch this,' she says, jumping off the wall, arms and legs wide apart. 'Hoshi jump!'

Eventually we make it to the station and, after buying our tickets, we've still got money left over. We both know what we want: food.

'Sushi!' says Hoshi.

'No way. Burger King!'

So we get both, and soon we're sitting opposite each other on the swaying train, sticking fries in soy sauce and sushi in ketchup. The carriage is almost empty, just some guy asleep against a window and a woman watching YouTube with her earphones in.

Hoshi takes the sachet of green stuff that came

with the sushi and rips it open. 'Ever tried wasabi before?'

'What is it?'

'Just something that tastes good with raw fish.'

'But we've eaten all the sushi.'

'We're going to have it on a fry.' She carefully squeezes the entire contents of the packet along two French fries.

'Looks like mushy peas,' I say.

'Tastes a bit different.' She hands me my chip. 'Are you ready?'

'Why? What does it do?' I stare at the thin strip of bright green paste.

'You'll see. On the count of three.' We hold our fries in front of our mouths. 'One . . . two . . . THREE!'

I stick it in my mouth in one go, just like Hoshi, and at first I just get this mustardy taste, but then then a fiery burn explodes in my mouth and shoots up my nostrils into my head. I yell and Hoshi laughs hysterically. 'Brain . . . exploding,' I gasp, then I shut my eyes because they're watering so much. 'Evil mustard's making me cry!'

She flops back in her seat. 'So funny . . . Evil mustard.' She holds up the other sachet of wasabi. 'Truth or dare?'

'Only if I can ask first,' I say, wiping my eyes with my sleeve.

Hoshi nods and I look out of the window at the lit-up houses flashing past while I think. I want to make my question count. I look back at her curled up in the corner of the seat. 'Why did you really leave Japan?' I say.

'Good question.' She twists a button on her cardi. 'I left Japan because of a kiss.'

'What?' I say. 'How can a *kiss* have made you leave?'

'No follow-up questions. My turn.' She throws me the wasabi. 'Sticking with the same theme . . .'

'Go on.'

'How many people have you ever kissed?'

I think about the parties I've been to, Friday nights I've spent hanging out in town, photos of me on Facebook that I hate but will never go away. Hoshi watches me from under the cap. 'I'll go with dare,' I say, ripping the wasabi packet open and sticking out my tongue.

'All of it,' she says.

I shrug and squeeze the burning paste into my mouth. My eyes shoot open, then the burn kicks in.

Back home we walk through the high street then out of town. Quite a few houses we go past have Christmas trees lit up in windows and flashing lights around doors. 'It's all wrong,' I say. 'It's not even December. Christmas stuff shouldn't happen yet.'

'I love it,' says Hoshi, gazing at a house covered in blue lights. 'This is going to be my first Christmas in England and Mum's coming. Dad used to visit us at Christmas and I'd spend the summers here.' She starts telling me about Christmas in Japan, how it's a bit like Valentine's day, with couples going out for romantic meals, and soon we get to the estate where she lives. It's all curving roads of quiet, perfect houses, with square lawns and cars parked on driveways. We stand together by a mini roundabout. 'Have you got far to go?' she asks.

'Not far. Won't your dad wonder where you've been?'

'He thinks I'm at your house,' she says. 'Your mum is dropping me home at eleven.' She looks at her phone. 'Hey, I'm early!'

'OK,' I say. I rock on my feet. Then I pull my hoodie closer to me as I think about my walk along the dual carriageway and the dark track to the farm.

'Thanks for busking with me,' Hoshi says.

'Thanks for being such a kickass dancer and getting us all that money.'

'That reminds me.' She opens up her purse and tips out some coins. 'I owe you your share of the change. There you go.'

I count the coins she's handed me. 'Thirty-two pence,' I say. 'I'll try not to spend it all at once.'

She starts to walk away. 'I'm glad you told me to get on the wrong train,' she says. 'Tonight was *sugoi*.'

'What's *sugoi*?'

'Awesome,' she says. Then, with a smile and a wave, she turns and heads down the dark road, the black cap bobbing up and down.

I watch her go, then start to walk out of town.

I hardly feel the cold and the taste of hot wasabi is still in my mouth. I think about Hoshi flipping through the air as the Japanese girls shouted, 'Hoshi! Hoshi!', and I think about what I just saw in her panda purse.

Three bank cards.

Why does a fifteen-year-old have *three* bank cards? And why did that fifteen-year-old make me go busking instead of using one of those cards to buy our tickets home? And then there's the mystery of the kiss that made her leave Japan . . .

A few days ago I'd have been thrilled to find this stuff out about Hoshi. It's just what I've been waiting for: evidence that she's a fake and that she's fooled everyone. But I'm not going to tell anyone.

Tonight Hoshi chose to let me see her dance – something she's kept hidden from everyone at school. She might have chosen to let me see her bank cards just then. I don't know why she trusts me, but it feels good.

Hoshi the secret agent, I think, my feet ringing on the deserted pavement. I'm glad she kept the cap. It suits her.

TWENTY-ONE

I'm standing high off the ground on a plank of wood balanced between two step ladders. Betty and Hoshi are next to me. We're rehearsing the famous balcony scene where Juliet leans out of her window and calls out, 'O Romeo, Romeo, wherefore art thou Romeo?' while Romeo hides behind some bushes, spying on her like a perv.

Right now, our Romeo is hiding behind a chair looking pretty fit in a grey short-sleeved shirt.

'Miss,' I say – the plank wobbles and I grab hold of Betty. 'Isn't it a bit weird that Tybalt and Mercutio are up on the balcony *with* Juliet?'

'You'll be in silhouette,' she says, looking up. 'No one will notice you.'

Ms Kapoor has decided that sixties-style backing singers are just what Romeo needs when he sings his solo, 'Ain't No Balcony High Enough'. For the past two hours, Betty and I have been singing, '*Doo-wop de doo da!*' on repeat.

'Jake, this time carry straight on with your lines,' says Ms Kapoor. 'Ready, girls?'

'Born ready,' says Betty, and Mr Simms starts playing the piano. We begin to sway from side to side, doo-wopping in unison, and Jake leaps out and starts to sing.

Watching us are Kat and Bea. It's been two weeks since I tried to abandon Hoshi in London and tonight me and the girls are going round to her place for a sleep-over. I glance at Hoshi and she smiles at me as she sings. A lot can happen in a fortnight.

We didn't tell the others what we did after their train left and this secret has stuck us together. When she walked into French on Monday, I pulled my books over and she sat next to me, the 'SECRET AGENT' cap pulled low on her head. Then she winked at me before stuffing the cap in her bag. Everything else followed on from that. We walked to R.S. together, met the girls at break, then hung out at lunchtime. Tiann didn't miss me because she's back with Max. As Hoshi and I live in the same direction, it seemed only natural to walk home together after Monday's rehearsal, and every other rehearsal after that.

And now we're having a sleepover. Unless you count crashing out on Tiann's sofa after drinking too much of her dad's home brew as a sleepover, I've not been to one for years.

The song finishes and Betty and I step to the side.

'"Romeo, Romeo, wherefore art thou Romeo?"' calls Hoshi, arms stretched out.

'"It is my lady,"' says Jake, '"O, it is my love! O, that she knew she were!"' Then their epic flirting session begins.

A couple of weeks ago, this would have been agony, especially as it's clear that Jake isn't acting when he gazes up at Hoshi and compares her eyes to twinkling stars. But since we went to London, those jealous feelings have been slipping away. That might be because I'm spending so much time with Hoshi: it's hard to be jealous of someone when it's you they want to hang around with. But even though we've been hanging out a lot, I still think she's keeping something hidden from me. That's one of the reasons I'm looking forward to tonight: you can tell a lot about someone from where they live.

'"O, wilt thou leave me so unsatisfied?"' asks Jake, then he climbs up a ladder towards us. It's supposed to be a drain pipe, but Miss says this will be sorted out when we get into the theatre. When he reaches us, he whispers, 'How you doin'?' to me and Betty. Each time he comes up here, he says something different to make us laugh.

'"What satisfaction canst thou have tonight?"' asks Hoshi. Then she persuades Romeo to marry her. Finally, after lots of hand holding and gazing, she says to Jake, '"I should *kill* thee with much cherishing."'

Her words echo round the room, deadly and sweet. Then, just as Ms Kapoor has instructed, she gives Jake a push and he falls dramatically off the ladder, rolling as he lands. Only this time, he keeps rolling until he ends up on Ms Kapoor's feet.

Miss stares down at him and Betty whispers in my ear, 'Lucky, lucky toes.' Then she cackles with laughter, the plank wobbles and the three of us grab each other as it tips forward and we're thrown to the ground.

'Move!' I say to Betty, who's lying on my leg.

'I can't. My hair's trapped under your fat bum!'

Ms Kapoor folds her arms and looks at us scattered across the stage. 'Let's call it a night,' she says.

TWENTY-TWO

'Dad!' calls Hoshi. 'We're home.'

We follow her into the house and even though we've been laughing the whole way here, driving each other crazy by saying 'Doo-wop de doo da' in answer to every single question, we all fall quiet, even Betty.

A man steps out of the kitchen. He's wearing a dark checked shirt and he's got specs and a beard, but it's a cool one, not an old man one. 'Hello,' he says, scratching his head. He's no blond.

'Dad, meet my friends,' says Hoshi. Then she introduces us and he nods at us in turn.

'I've got some food in for you,' he says, pulling on his trainers. 'I didn't know what you like or if any of you are vegetarian, so I bought lots of different things.' He grabs a jacket and then pats his pockets until he finds his keys. 'Have fun,' he says. 'I'll be back around eleven.' He smiles quickly, then disappears out of the door.

'Sorry about that,' says Hoshi. 'Dad's –'

'Really hot?' says Kat, eyes wide.

'What? No!' Hoshi kicks off her shoes. 'I was going to say he's shy.'

'He's young and handsome, but he's a dad,' says Kat. 'Really confusing . . .'

We take off our shoes, then follow Hoshi into the kitchen. 'Dad was only twenty when he had me,' she says. 'He met Mum when he was in Japan teaching English.' She starts pulling stuff out of the Sainsbury's bags on the table.

'When did they split up?' I ask.

Hoshi looks at me and smiles. For a second I'm sure she knows I'm digging around for information. 'They were never really together. Dad came back to England and Mum stayed in Japan with me.' We start to help her with the shopping. 'What's this?' she says, pulling a whole chicken out of the bag. 'He hasn't got a clue! Why didn't he just get pizza?'

'Let's see,' says Betty, rummaging in another bag. 'Hash browns, dim sum, mince pies, strawberries . . .'

Hoshi holds up a bag of Haribo bears. 'He's bought all my favourite food.'

'So sweet,' says Kat. 'Look, Petits Filous!'

'I liked them when I was *five*. Dad doesn't know me that well.'

'He's got us *wine*!' says Bea. 'And strawberry milk powder.'

'Does he know how old you are?' asks Betty, picking up the bottle.

'Not sure,' says Hoshi, putting a can of Peppa Pig spaghetti next to the chicken. 'Come on. I'll show you the rest of the house.'

There's hardly any furniture in the front room – just a futon, some cushions and the biggest TV I've ever seen. Attached to it is a PlayStation 4 and two handsets. 'Dad only moved in here when he knew I was coming,' says Hoshi, looking around. 'His old place was too small.'

Betty is looking through the pile of games on the

floor. '*Bloodborne . . . Call of Duty . . . Gran Turismo 7 . . .*' she says. 'I want your dad!'

'Let's go upstairs,' says Hoshi. 'We can play later.'

I let the others go first and take my time following them. All the walls are painted creamy white, like milk, and there are no carpets – just shiny laminate floor that's slippery under my socks. At the bottom of the stairs is a pile of post and on the top is a postcard of a Manga girl wearing shorts and twirling an umbrella. I reach down to pick it up.

'There you are,' says Hoshi, her head appearing round the banister. 'We're all in my room.' I leave the postcard and follow her upstairs.

Hoshi's got the biggest bedroom and, just like the rest of the house, there's not much furniture: just a desk, a couple of posters and another futon. 'It's like a dance studio,' says Bea, twirling in the empty space.

Kat flops down on the mattress. 'This is cool. I like being this low down.'

'I'd rather have a proper bed,' says Hoshi, 'but Dad is big into Japanese culture. He's more into it than Mum.'

I go to look at some photos on the window sill. Behind me, music comes on and the girls laugh at something Betty's said. I pick up a heart-shaped frame and Hoshi comes over. 'That's me and Mum,' she says. I look at the small smiling lady wearing a red dress and holding a fat baby with one dimple. 'Dad had already gone back to England then. You don't get that many single mums in Japan. Luckily my nan and granddad are very cool and helped her out.'

'Are these your friends?' I pick up the next photo. Four girls stand side by side, their arms linked, wearing identical checked skirts, knee-high socks and white jumpers.

'Yep. My friends back home.'

'No. Way!' Kat shouts. We turn round to see she's disappeared inside a cupboard. 'My ultimate dream: a walk-in wardrobe. Girls, you have to see this.'

Betty and Bea follow her inside and I can hear them oohing and aahing. 'Hoshi,' says Bea, sticking her head out. She's got a tiny, glittery top hat balanced on her curly hair. 'Your clothes are *insane*.'

They start pulling things out to show me: polka-dot frilly skirts, sequinned waistcoats, candy-coloured trainers. 'How many pairs of stripy knee-high socks does one girl need?' asks Betty, searching through a plastic bag.

'About seventeen?' says Hoshi with a laugh.

I push past Betty and squeeze into the wardrobe next to Kat and Bea. I run my hands over a blue frilly dress covered in unicorns and lace. 'How come you never wear any of this stuff?' I ask.

'Because everyone would laugh at me,' says Hoshi, peering in. 'Can you imagine me walking down the high street in that?'

I pull out a lacy tartan skirt. 'So did you wear this in Tokyo?'

'Only if I wanted to dress up.' We all start trying on Hoshi's clothes and she tells us about the different looks in Japan. 'I'm mainly a Decora girl, but occasionally I do a bit of Sweet Lolita.'

'Nice,' says Kat, nodding like she knows exactly what Hoshi's on about.

'Explain,' I say as I try to squeeze my feet into a pair of pastel pink lace-up boots.

'Decora is about bright colours and wearing tons of *kawaii* accessories – cartoon hair grips, that sort of thing. *Kawaii* means "cute". Sweet Lolita is basically short frilly dresses. Usually they're pink. Oh, and curly wigs.'

'Found a wig!' shouts Bea, who still hasn't come out of the wardrobe.

'Bea, have you looked in the mirror recently?' says Betty. 'That wig is basically your hair . . . but purple.'

Hoshi sits on the futon watching as we parade around in her clothes. She's wearing baggy jeans, an oversized T-shirt and a pink cartoon whale necklace. I now realise this is the most normal she can possibly look.

'Stop,' says Kat, pulling off a silver wig. 'I'm hungry. Who can cook whole chickens?'

It turns out I'm the only person who can cook whole chickens.

'Stick it in the oven,' says Kat. 'Let's have a dinner party!'

TWENTY-THREE

Two hours later, the chicken is ready. I've done the cooking (wearing the unicorn dress), Hoshi's laid the table and sorted out the music, and Bea (wearing a pink tartan mini skirt and white furry boots) has lit the candles. Our dinner party is basically everything Hoshi's dad bought. Once we've put it all on the table it looks like a crazy feast with bowls of sweets sitting next to a pile of hash browns and mince pies.

'Can we have the wine?' asks Betty. Somehow she's managed to squeeze into a tiny pair of white dungarees.

'I don't like wine,' says Kat.

'Me neither,' says Bea.

'I'm having strawberry milk,' says Hoshi, filling up a glass with milk.

'Well, I know someone who won't say no,' says Betty, wiggling the bottle in my direction.

I look at the bottle and think about all the Friday nights Tiann and I have gone to the rec with everyone else and then shared a bottle of wine, waiting for something to happen. I shake my head. 'I'll go with pink milk,' I say.

Betty puts the bottle down. 'You're all boring,' she says, holding out her glass for some milk.

We eat the chicken with the Peppa Pig spaghetti, then dip strawberries in the Petits Filous. When Betty says the dim sum look like 'lonely boobies', Bea laughs so much that yogurt actually comes out of her nose.

'I'd forgotten how mad your laugh is, Bea,' I say.

'Missed it?'

I nod. 'Just a bit.'

After we've tidied up, we play *Gran Turismo*, but when Hoshi's dad comes in, we go up to her room. She pulls out airbeds and sleeping bags, and her dad brings up the mattress from the futon downstairs and soon her room is basically one giant bed.

We lie in the dark, talking and laughing. This might be my first sleepover in a while, but nothing's changed. We talk about school, boys, clothes, and anything that comes into our heads, but gradually our voices become whispers and first Bea falls asleep, followed by the others.

I lie on my back, staring at the ceiling and listening to the soft breathing all around me.

'Hey,' a voice whispers, then a cuddly toy bounces off my face. 'You awake?'

I roll over. Hoshi is half sitting up, her chin resting in her hands, her hair making a halo round her head. 'I am now.' I throw the toy back at her.

'We don't really have sleepovers in Japan.' Her voice drifts towards me. 'I bet you guys have loads.'

I laugh. 'They might have had them, but I wasn't invited.'

'How come?'

'When we were little,' I say, 'the four of us had sleepovers all the time, mainly at Betty's. Sometimes I'd stay there the whole weekend . . . But then we all fell out.'

She wriggles round in the bed so that she's closer to me. 'What made you fall out?'

I try to think how I can sum up years and years of fights and arguments. What did happen to stop me going round to Betty's with the others? How did we go from sharing everything to not speaking?

'We had nothing in common,' I say. 'I found them boring.' My words fall into the dark room where my friends are all sleeping. I feel my cheeks flush. 'No, that wasn't it. It was my fault. I wasn't exactly a good friend.' I feel hot. I unzip the sleeping bag. I don't want to talk about this any more. It's been better between me and the girls since we went to London, but Bea's words on the train unlocked something in my mind and I'm finding I can't push things away like I used to.

'But now you're back together,' says Hoshi.

'Almost,' I say. 'Did you know we met at nursery school and we had a secret club?'

Hoshi laughs. 'What were you called?'

'The Ladybirds. We'd do this all day across the

classroom.' I tuck in my thumb and wiggle my four fingers at her.

She wiggles hers back. 'That's sweet. I've not been friends with anyone for that long.'

'What about your friends in the photo?'

'Oh, them.' I can just make out her smile. 'I've not seen them for ages.'

'Did you move?'

In the corner of the room, Bea rolls over, throwing her arms above her head. 'I stopped going to that school,' Hoshi says. She sits up. 'It's almost been a perfect sleepover, but I did want a pillow fight and a midnight feast.'

I pull my pillow out and swing it at her head. She tries to duck, but I hit her smack in the face. 'There,' I say. 'You've had a pillow fight.'

She chucks the pillow back at me. 'I thought it would go on for longer.'

'I'm tired. Go to sleep.'

She flops back in bed.

'Night, Pearl.'

'Night, Hoshi.'

I roll over and stare at the shadows on the cupboard door. Gradually, the breathing around me gets deeper and Betty starts to snore. I shift around on my airbed, trying to find a cool spot then I sit up and turn over my pillow. Hoshi is buried under her duvet, just the top of her head sticking out.

'Hoshi?' I whisper. No reply.

I wriggle out of the sleeping bag, tiptoe across the room and along the corridor. Hoshi's dad's door is shut and his light is off. I stand still. It's almost totally dark and so quiet. In my house, there's always a light or TV on; Mum keeps her radio on all night.

I go downstairs, treading gently on each step, and find the postcard. Moonlight streams in from the window above the door and I see that the cartoon girl has a key ring hanging off her belt – a rainbow rabbit – and the umbrella is covered in flowers.

A ticking noise makes me look up. I stare into the darkness upstairs until the noise stops, then turn the postcard over. Everything is in Japanese, except the address. 'Hoshi Kita,' it says, '6 Turney Crescent'. Not Hoshi Lockwood. I store 'Hoshi Kita' away with all Hoshi's other little secrets, then put the postcard back where I found it.

I drift around the kitchen, opening and shutting drawers until I find a packet of Kit Kats. I sit on the worktop and snap off one stick, eating it in a couple of bites and washing it down with some water.

Back upstairs, I put the other half of the Kit Kat on Hoshi Kita's pillow and climb into my sleeping bag. I wrapped it back up in its silver foil so it won't melt on her face. Now she's got a midnight feast.

TWENTY-FOUR

On Saturday I hang out with Tiann for a couple of hours and Sunday is spent dipping my hands into the freezing carp tank at World of Water. 'Frozen fish fingers,' I say to Jane, holding up my blue fingers. She collapses with laughter – it's so easy to make my boss laugh. Then she starts telling me about her night out in Hastings at a wine bar called Jailhouse Rock.

'As soon as you're eighteen, I'll take you,' she says, plunging her arms back into the water. She pulls up a handful of slimy black stuff from the bottom of the tank and drops it in the bucket. 'The owner was dressed as Elvis. He sang "Love Me Tender" to me.' She smiles at the memory and I flick fishy water at her.

'Come on,' she says. 'Let's tidy up, then I'll drop you home.'

When I get in, the house is empty, so I go straight to my room and start to clean out my tank. I hate doing it when Mum and Alfie are around because they don't understand about the water – it needs to stay sterile. I take some of the old stuff out, making sure I don't suck any fish up through the suction tube, and then I go to the kitchen and start to fill the bucket with fresh water, sprinkling salt mix in as I go.

Alfie comes in as I'm running the hot tap and staring at the digital thermometer. 'Alright?' I say, glancing up.

'Yep,' he says, and Callum walks in behind him. He's the only friend either of us ever has back.

'Hey,' says Callum with a quick nod. I got off with him once. Big mistake. I can't stand even looking at him now. He's got eyes that bulge like a blenny's.

'Where's Mum?' asks Alfie.

'Stables.' I check my bucket.

'I need twenty quid,' he says to my back. I look at the

thermometer. Nearly there. I turn off the hot tap and add some cold. 'Can you lend it to me?'

'No,' I say, swirling the thermometer round and round in the black bucket. 'Sorry.'

He goes over to the fridge and looks inside. 'You know Bobby in your year?'

'Everyone knows Bobby,' I say.

'His brother's got a bike that he's scrapping. Says I can have the engine parts, but I need to get him the money today.'

'Mum's definitely up at the stables.'

'If you lend it to me, you can get it back off her. Do you want a Coke?' he asks Callum, then he chucks a can to him. Callum, like an idiot, opens it straight away and the drink sprays in his face.

Alfie laughs and Callum shakes the can in his direction. 'Nice, mate. Tesco Value!'

'Don't drink it if you don't want it,' says Alfie. Coke hits the back of my neck and I lean over my bucket, trying to stop any from going in the water.

'Sorry, Pearl,' says Alfie, still laughing. He must really

want that money. He knows I get paid in cash every Sunday, but that would be half my money gone. No way would Mum pay me back.

'C'mon,' says Callum, heading through to the lounge. 'Let's play *FIFA*.'

'Set it up,' says Alfie. I turn the tap on a bit more. Alfie is somewhere behind me, but all I can hear is the whirring of the fridge and the water hitting the bucket. Hairs on the back of my neck prickle. 'Go on. Lend us the twenty.' He's crept closer.

'Just go and ask Mum,' I say. 'She's five minutes away.'

Twenty-six degrees. I turn off the tap. Alfie is totally silent. I get ready to haul the bucket out of the sink, then a thin trickle of brown liquid comes down in front of my face and into the water. Alfie moves the can of Coke slightly so that it trickles over my hair and sleeve.

I freeze and hold my breath. 'Whoops,' he says. Then he drops the can into the sink with a clatter.

I want to pick up the can and throw it in his face, but I know it would be a mistake. 'Alfie!' shouts Callum from the lounge. 'I'm Villa.'

'Coming,' he says, walking away, and I release my grip on the bucket, tip the water out and start all over again.

Back in my room, water changed and pH and salinity levels checked, I turn on my laptop and put on Sub FM. The bang of the front door tells me Alfie and Callum have gone out. My shoulders relax.

Outside it's pitch-black, but I don't bother turning on any lights. I like it dark.

I think about going on YouTube, but instead I type 'dancing Japan' into Google. I feel like I'm spying on Hoshi, but I want to see if I can make sense of some of her secrets. All the results are in Japanese, so I switch to images, and photos of ladies in kimonos and white tights fill the screen. Next I try searching for 'street dance Japan' and then 'dancing singing Japan'.

I spend half an hour scrolling through pictures of dancing teenagers and watching a few films, but I've not found what I'm looking for. A moving shadow on the screen makes me swing round and stare hard at the window. I know the shifting shapes are only trees, but I still have to get up and pull the curtains shut.

I settle back on the floor in front of my laptop. 'Hoshi Kita' I type. It's what I should have tried straight away.

A list of results written in Japanese appear, but at the bottom of the page I see one written in English. It's a Wattpad profile of teenager called Hoshi Kita. 'Likes: Piano, touring, people, bunnies. Dislikes: Dead things, hospital, mean people.' There's a thumbnail picture of a Japanese girl, but it's definitely not Hoshi.

I switch back to images and suddenly the screen is filled with tiny photos of Japanese girls. None of them have messy pink bobs. Then a girl clutching a sunflower catches my eye. She has copper ringlets and almond eyes. I enlarge the picture and suddenly Hoshi is staring straight at me, head tilted to one side. I hold my breath. The girl is covered in make-up, but it's definitely Hoshi. She's even got a dimple in her left cheek.

Now I know to look for a girl with copper curls, I realise Hoshi is in lots of the pictures. Sometimes she's alone – blowing a kiss, laughing, peeking out from behind her fingers – but in most of the photos she's posing with a group of other girls. I click on one of them at random. Some girls are lined up against a brick wall, wearing a mix of cheerleading skirts, vests, shorts and stripy knee-high socks. Hoshi is in the centre, arms folded, leaning against another girl. Her socks are purple and pink striped. Betty was wearing those socks on Friday night!

Every girl in the photo has 'Baby Girlz' written across her chest. A quick check on Wikipedia tells me that the Baby Girlz are a Japanese idol group – a huge pop group made up of sixty girls who perform in different teams. I stare at the screen and blink: Hoshi is a pop star!

Even though the idea is bizarre – and pop star Hoshi looks so different to the one I know – it also explains so much. Not just her amazing singing and dancing, but also her confidence. One photo, taken from the back of the stage, shows Hoshi and her group smiling at the camera. Behind them is a mass of people and they're all clapping and screaming. No wonder she just accepts attention.

'Fish and chips!' comes a shout from outside my door. I didn't even hear Mum come in.

'Coming!' I call, my eyes running over the Baby Girlz videos I've found on YouTube. I click on one and Hoshi springs to life, dancing with her group. It's so carefully synchronised that the girls seem to form a single moving shape.

'They're getting cold,' says Mum. 'I'll leave yours on the table.' Then I hear her clumping upstairs followed by Ozzie's padding feet.

I don't get up. I need to know more.

I type Hoshi's name into YouTube along with Baby Girlz. The same videos appear, but one of them looks different. It's weird. Hoshi's head is shaved and her head is bowed forward. 'Shamed idol' says the caption. I press play.

Hoshi looks up at the camera, eyes wide. She's sitting in front of a blue wall wearing a bright white sweat-shirt. With her shaved head she looks like she's sick. Her ears stick out from her head and tufts of hair show what a bad job someone's made with the razor. She whispers to the camera in Japanese and, as she speaks, tears start to roll down her cheeks. I feel my cheeks flush because I don't think she's acting and I hate hearing her shaking voice. She bows deeply, once, twice, then her face crumples and she's crying so hard that she can't even talk.

I snap the laptop shut.

My music is still playing and I can hear the wind outside. A branch taps on my window. That trembling person wasn't Hoshi. Someone must have made her do it!

For weeks, I wanted to see her smile wiped off her face, but now it's happened . . . Just the thought of her whispering voice makes me feel sick.

'Pearl!' shouts Mum from the top of the stairs. 'Food. Now!'

TWENTY-FIVE

I sit in French waiting for Hoshi to turn up. She wasn't on the bus. Instead, I got Tiann telling me about Tynan's worms, and a little bit more time to work out what I'm going to say to Hoshi.

All last night, my laptop sat in the corner of my room, but I didn't touch it. Instead, I ate cold fish and chips, listened to music and read a book Mum left lying around. But I couldn't stop seeing Hoshi's bowing head.

'Hey!' Hoshi says, making me jump.

'Where've you been?' I ask as she slips into the seat next to me.

'Dad dropped me off, but I couldn't get him ready on time.' She pulls off her cardi and I see a fake tattoo of an owl on her wrist. 'He's hopeless. He was actually going to go to work with Weetabix in his beard.'

A worksheet is put on the desk in front of us. '*Jobs de Rêve*,' I say, reading out the title. 'Dream jobs . . . What's yours, Hoshi? I've got to write it in this box.' I tap the pen on the sheet. 'Magician . . . actor . . . *pop star*?'

She looks up from her bag. 'I don't know . . . designer?' She pulls out her pencil case. 'What's your dream job?'

'Detective,' I say.

That's how it is all day. I ask Hoshi about music in Japan, her favourite bands, what she listens to, and she just looks me in the eye and answers all my questions. By the time we go to our rehearsal, I've realised that she isn't going to tell me about the Baby Girlz. I don't know why it's such a secret, but I think it must have something to do with that video. And that kind of makes me feel bad for pushing her.

We're just singing today, going over the songs. We've learnt them all now and we're sorting out the harmonies.

Hoshi and I sit in the back row with the girls and Jake. He loves it, especially as he's next to Hoshi.

To start with, we're well behaved, but while the tenors are working on their part in 'Capulet It Go', Bea puts a photo of us on Facebook. It was taken at her seventh birthday and I'm wearing a pink leotard and I've got something stuck to my forehead. I'm supposed to be a unicorn, but Gran really screwed up the horn. Betty doesn't look much better. She's wearing beige tights and nothing else. Her hair is bright green and backcombed into a twist on top of her head.

'What was the theme?' whispers Kat.

'Magical creatures,' says Bea. 'I'm a fairy.'

'What's Betty supposed to be?' I ask. 'A naked freak?'

'Like you can talk,' Betty says. 'What's that on your head?'

'A horn! I was a unicorn.'

'Well, it doesn't look like a horn, and you don't look like a unicorn,' says Betty. 'Obviously, I was a troll.'

Soon we're laughing so much that Mr Simms separates us and I end up at the front, right under his nose.

I still manage to text, **You da naked freak** to Betty before he snatches my phone off me.

As usual, Hoshi and I walk home together. We cut across the park. It's dark, but lamp posts line the path and we walk in and out of their circles of light. A dog with long skinny legs runs up and sniffs my hand. I give its ears a stroke, but a whistle from the trees makes it bound away.

I smoke a cigarette while we walk. To begin with we chat about the show – we've reached the point where all the scenes are slotting together and we can almost see how good it's going to be – then a woman walks past in a fluffy coat and Hoshi goes off on one about snow monkeys. 'Dad took me to see them when he was visiting,' she says, doing a few extra steps to keep up with me. 'We travelled into the mountains to a monkey park and there they were, grey monkeys all chillaxing in the hot pools, lounging about, eyes half shut, looking like my Japanese granddad. You'd love them, Pearl.'

'Monkeys are cool,' I say.

'And they play in the snow. Did I tell you about the squirrel fighting the carp?'

'Yes . . . and the massive spider crab.' I grind my fag into the top of a bin. 'Enough nature, Hoshi.' I stop walking. 'Tell me about something else.'

She turns to face me. She's all bundled up in a puffy silver coat. 'What?' she says.

'Idol groups. They're big in Japan, aren't they?'

She spins round and walks towards the playground. 'Coming?' she calls over her shoulder as she jumps the fence.

When I get to the swings, she's already swinging up and down, leaning right back and staring at the dark, cloudy sky. I stand in front of her, arms folded. 'Aren't you going to swing?' she says. Then she takes a deep breath through her nose. 'It smells like snow!'

'Tell me about idol groups, Hoshi.'

'They're stupid manufactured pop groups,' she says. 'Perfect girls sing songs that mean *nothing*. I hate them!' She shouts this out.

'What about Baby Girlz?' I say. The wind blows dry leaves across the playground. 'Do you hate them?'

Hoshi lets her legs drop down and she comes to a stop. 'Yeah. They're the worst.' She looks at me and laughs. 'Clever Pearl,' she says. 'When did you work it out?'

'Only last night,' I say, sitting on the swing next to her. The chains are icy cold.

'Have you told anyone?' She stares at me.

'No.'

'Good.' We both watch as a woman jogs past the playground.

'So . . . are you famous?' I ask.

'Only in Japan.'

'Famous enough for those girls in London to know who you were.'

'That was bad luck,' she says. 'Come on. Let's see who can go highest.' She starts to swing again and I join in. The woman has gone and now we're on our own, swinging up and down, our feet moving in unison. 'Baby Girlz is a young group – everyone's under eighteen,' she says, 'and the team I was in did this mad acrobatic dancing – all synchronised. I performed with them for a year.'

'How come you stopped?'

She glances across at me. 'If you did your research properly, Pearl, then I'm sure you've seen the video.'

'I saw it, but I didn't get it.'

'I got kicked out of the Baby Girlz because I was caught kissing some boy and that's against the group rules.'

'The kiss that made you leave,' I say. Leaves blow down from the tree above us, falling all around us as we swing.

'That's it.'

'But that's stupid.'

'We were supposed to be perfect.' She reaches out and tries to catch a leaf with her hand. 'We weren't allowed to date in case it ruined our image. Anyway, someone took photos of us kissing – you'll find them online if you look hard enough – and I was thrown out of the band.'

'Who was he?' I say. Then I slow down. I'm starting to feel dizzy.

'No one.' Hoshi slows down too and our feet scuff the ground. 'That's the funny thing.' She laughs. 'I didn't even like him, but I still got chucked out!'

'So you made the film.'

She groans. 'What a mistake. Some of the other girls thought it might work and I was so desperate to stay in the band that I did it.' Hoshi stops her swing and looks at me. 'I begged the fans to forgive me and put the film on YouTube. Then the press went crazy.'

'How come you ended up here?' I say. I can't stop asking questions now. 'Can you actually get thrown out of Japan for kissing?'

She laughs. 'Mum and Dad wanted me to try "ordinary life" for a while. Once I realised I wasn't getting back into the Girlz, I agreed. So here I am . . . being ordinary!'

'Busking at Covent Garden . . . starring in the school musical . . .'

'Yeah. I'm a show off.' She grins.

'Come on, then.'

'What?'

I give her puffy shoulder a push. 'Let's hear a Baby Girlz song.'

'What? Here?'

'Don't be shy. How many people used to go to your gigs?'

'We performed at the Yokohama Arena to seventeen thousand.'

'So performing for one should be easy.'

Hoshi jumps off the swing. 'I'll do the song with the most English in it,' she says, '"Kiss! Kiss! Kiss!"'

'Is it about kissing?'

'Ha ha.' She turns her back on me and raises one fist to the black sky. 'Ready?' she says over her shoulder.

I lean on the chain. 'Ready.'

She spins round and starts to dance. Just like in London, she's slick and fast, but this time a huge smile is stuck on her face. '*K-I-S-S, K-I-S-S, K-I-S-S, kissing with you!*' she sings, then she pouts and does a series of air kisses. 'Then I did a scream,' she says, 'because I was "the wacky one".' She screams a delicate scream then flips over backwards, and starts singing 'K-I-S-S!' all over again before switching to Japanese. The dance is full of flips, but her face never shows that she's putting much effort into them. The whole time she looks relaxed and thrilled to be dancing her ass off in a cold, windy park.

She finishes by jumping into the air and yelling a final 'Kiss!' I clap and watch as her huge smile disappears and a more normal Hoshi-sized one appears in its place. Over by the fence a lady is staring at us, a poo bag dangling from one hand and a little dog yapping round her heels.

'Cheesy?' says Hoshi, raising one eyebrow.

'Totally . . . but who cares? You're a real pop star!'

Hoshi shivers. The wind has picked up. 'Come on,' she says. 'Let's go.'

We leave the playground and walk through the park and past the locked tennis courts. Hoshi tells me about all the weird stuff she used to have to do. 'Fans would pay to meet us in a booth,' she says, 'and, one time, we filmed a video in the middle of winter and they made us wear bikinis. We had to suck ice cubes so we didn't have frosty breath when we sang.'

'What was it like being famous?' I ask.

'Awesome . . . to begin with. I could make someone's day just by looking at them.' She snaps a twig off a bush and starts running it along the wall. 'But I got tired of having to be good and being told how to act. I was faking it all the time and in the end that makes you miserable.' We're nearly out of the park now, walking down a gravelly path. 'But now I'm happy,' she adds.

'Walking past a dog poo bin in the rain?'

'Rain?' She sticks her hand out. 'I really thought it was going to snow!' We walk on in the icy drizzle, then she says, 'You won't tell anyone, will you?'

'Why's it such a big secret?'

'Mum and Dad were right. It's better being normal.'

'I won't tell anyone,' I say. We come out of the park by Tesco Express, then wait for the lights to change at the crossing. '*K-I-S-S* . . . ' I sing under my breath.

'*Pearl!*'

'What? I can't help it. It's so catchy.' Then the green man comes on and – in time to the beeps – I sing Hoshi's song at the top of my voice and dance across the road.

'Shut up,' she yells, hitting me with her bag, but I sing it all the way to the mini roundabout. 'When am I going to come back to your place?' she asks. 'I want to meet your fish.' I've shown Hoshi loads of films of Oy swimming around. Her face lights up. 'Why don't I come back now?'

'No way,' I say. 'My room's a mess, and my house is right out of town. You'd need a lift home.'

'My dad could pick me up.' I try to imagine Hoshi picking her way between the bags of dog food as I lead her to my room, her face when she sees the lock on my door.

'Maybe another day,' I say. 'I've got to go.' I turn and walk down the road. 'K-I-S-S!' I call over my shoulder.

'S-H-U-T-U-P!' she shouts. I know she's still looking at me, so I do her signature 'cheeky jump', my fist punching the drizzly sky, and her mad laugh follows me down the road.

TWENTY-SIX

I'm good at keeping Hoshi's secret. We're getting so close to opening night now, rehearsing every other day, and it's fun watching Hoshi pretend not to be a pop star. Whenever she asks Ms Kapoor to help her with a simple move or she struggles over her harmonies, she glances over at me and we share a look, just for a second, and she knows her secret is safe with me.

After Thursday's rehearsal, Kat walks home with us. It's freezing, but Miss worked us so hard we don't really feel it. As we walk, we talk about the show and Christmas, and how we can't believe we break up next Friday. Mr Simms turned up tonight dressed as Father Christmas and gave us all presents: Santa hats that either had Capulet or Montague written on them. We wore them all through the rehearsal and they kept flying off whenever we did anything acrobatic.

'I'm sorry, Pearl,' says Kat, interrupting me, 'but when are you going to mention Evie's crop top?'

'What?' I think back to what Evie was wearing. 'Oh yeah. A bit tacky.'

'*Tacky?* That's it? She had "I wish my brains were this big" written across her boobs. When she did that solo shimmy, I thought you were going to destroy her.'

I shrug and push my hands into my blazer pockets. 'I guess I didn't notice.'

'Too busy dancing,' says Hoshi.

'I don't know.' Kat looks at me through narrowed eyes. 'You're being way too nice these days, Pearl. It's giving me the creeps.'

'I'm always nicer when I'm in a show. I'm not so bored.'

'Still . . .' she says. '"I wish my brains were this big"!'

'I get to be horrible on stage,' I say. 'Get it out of my system. Tonight was fun.' After we'd learnt the dance, we ran through the scene we're doing tomorrow – the big fight between Romeo, Tybalt and Mercutio, when

Betty and I are murdered. We're a bit bummed out to die halfway through the play, so Miss is resurrecting us for the chorus line. She says she can't afford to kill off two of her best singers.

'I'm coming to watch tomorrow,' says Hoshi.

'Me too,' says Kat, then she nudges me. 'Seeing you wrestle Jake Flower is going to be so memorable. I bet you can't wait!'

I laugh. 'I've not really thought about it.'

'I don't believe that!' says Kat.

'It's true! Maybe it's because I'm seeing so much of him at rehearsals; it's making me immune to the power of his face.'

'As if!' Kat says. 'The gap, Pearl, what about his tooth gap?'

'Bit too gappy?'

She shakes her head. 'No such thing.'

I glance over at Hoshi. Although we talk about everything now, Jake seems to be off limits. 'Anyway,' I say, suddenly curious to see what she really thinks of him, 'everyone knows he fancies Hoshi.'

A silence falls over us, then Hoshi laughs and says. 'No, he doesn't!'

'*Yes*, he does,' says Kat, clearly delighted to be able to talk about this at last. 'Jake told me you were "as cute as a button"!'

Hoshi shakes her head. 'He says stuff like that about everyone. He's a massive flirt. He told me Pearl was "magnetic" on the stage.'

Kat gasps and grabs Hoshi's arm. 'What's he said about me?'

She thinks for a second, then says, 'Oh, when you were playing the ukelele the other day, he said it made your hands look massive, like a giant's.'

Kat stares at her hands. 'Not what I was hoping to hear, Hoshi . . .'

We separate at the roundabout and I walk home in the dark, shouting my lines out loud to the cars that fly past along the dual carriageway. I must look crazy, but I don't care. '"Thou art a villain"!' I say to a Primark van; '"Wretched boy",' I hiss at a battered Range Rover.

When I get to the footpath that leads to the farm, I

sing for the cows that are standing still and silent, like statues. First I do 'Capulet It Go', then the chorus of 'Kiss! Kiss! Kiss!' It really is catchy.

As I'm walking past the next field, I find one of the horses, Tonto, standing by the fence. He arrived at the stables years ago and I spent hours training him with Mum. I liked pretending he was my horse. We look at each other for a moment and I take in his huge beautiful eyes. 'Haven't you got big?' I say, holding out my hand to him. He takes a step closer. 'Mum not put you away yet?'

With a sudden flick of his tail, he turns and walks towards the shadowy trees. 'It's me,' I call after him, 'Pearl!' but he doesn't turn back.

I let myself into the kitchen, dump my bag on the floor and start hunting for food. Since Mum's last big shop she's just brought milk and bread from the garage, but I find crackers at the back of a cupboard and some chocolate spread. I make a pile of cracker sandwiches and carry them into my room.

I put music on and feed my fish, kicking clothes and

shoes out of the way as I go round my room. A slammed door followed by thundering paws and a series of barks tells me Mum's home. This is my chance to do my solo for her. I couldn't show her last night because Alfie was around.

'Mum,' I call as I go down the corridor. I stop in the doorway to the front room. It's not her sprawled across the sofa: it's Alfie. He's flicking through channels and pushing Ozzie away with his foot. 'Where's Mum?' I say.

'She's gone out with a friend so I had to get Ozzie.'

'When's she back?'

Alfie shrugs and points the control at the TV. He's choosing a film. 'Late.'

'Watch that,' I say. Alfie has stopped on *Ted*. 'It's funny.' As soon as I say this, he goes back to the main menu. This makes me laugh.

'What,' he says, scowling.

'Nothing.' I lean over the back of the sofa. I'm not going to let him bring me down tonight. He picks another film at random, something about a soldier in

Iraq, and soon I find myself sitting on the beanbag and watching it with him. I only plan to stay for five minutes, but soon I'm gripped.

'I'm going to do that,' he says, pointing at the screen. A soldier is firing a machine gun at a dusty bank. 'As soon as I'm eighteen.' Alfie's always wanted to join the army, but you need parental consent if you're under eighteen and Mum won't let him. It's the main thing they argue about. Alfie takes a cigarette out of the pack on the table and lights it. 'Want one?' he asks, pushing the pack towards me.

I stare at him. He rolls his eyes. 'Do you want a fag or not?'

'Thanks.' Quickly I take a cigarette and Alfie chucks his lighter at me. Officially, I'm not allowed to smoke, so I never do it in front of Mum, but school's internally excluded me for it so many times she must know I do it.

A tank explodes and Ozzie tries to jump up on the sofa next to Alfie. 'You stink,' he says, pushing her away. She just tries to lick his face.

'Don't let Mum hear you say that.'

Alfie actually smiles, just for a second. 'The other day,' he says, 'I saw her brushing Ozzie with your hair brush.'

'What? I found it full of grey hairs, but I thought they were Mum's!' Alfie laughs and Ozzie's tail curls under. She comes over to me and sniffs my ear. I rub the top of her head. 'Smelly dog,' I whisper.

We smoke and watch the film for a few more minutes, then I say, 'Hey, Alfie, you know on Monday when it rained?' He nods without taking his eyes off the screen. 'Well, Mum used the shirt you're wearing to dry Ozzie.' His eyes narrow in disgust and I laugh. 'She was soaked!'

He sits up with a jerk, pulls off his shirt, scrunches it into a ball and chucks it at me.

'Sorry,' I say, but now I'm laughing even more.

'Shut up,' he says.

But I've got the giggles and I can't stop. 'Did you wear it to college?' I ask. He turns to look at me; his eyes narrow. I stop laughing. 'Sorry,' I say.

But it's too late.

He pulls back his arm and hurls the TV control at

me. Ozzie yelps and I turn my face, just as the control smacks into my forehead and falls on to the floor. My hands fly up and I press my fingers down to stop the stinging pain. 'God . . .' I sit still, waiting for the sick dizziness to fade. Slowly, hands in front of my face, I look up to see if he's going to do anything else.

He's staring at the TV. 'I told you to shut up,' he mutters.

I take my fingers away and see a smear of blood. My head throbs. I wipe my hand on the beanbag. 'They'll *never* have you in the army,' I whisper. It's the worst thing I can think to say to him.

'If you tell Mum . . .'

I shake my head. 'I won't.' Ozzie presses into my legs. Through her silky hair I can feel her heart beating wildly. I hug her to me. 'It's OK,' I whisper.

TWENTY-SEVEN

I don't tell Mum. Instead, I get up a bit earlier so I can hide the bruise with make-up. My head aches, but I do a good job and Mum doesn't notice when we pass in the kitchen.

I doodle all the way through drama and biology, then I'm with Hoshi for geography. 'Why are you so quiet?' she asks.

'Just thinking,' I say.

'What about?'

'Fighting.'

'Not long until the rehearsal,' she says with a smile. 'Ready to die?'

'As long as I get to finish this first,' I say, and I go back to colouring in my diagram of river landforms.

★

It's a small rehearsal – the Friday night ones usually are – just Jake, Betty and me. Hoshi and Kat have come along to watch, but Bea's gone late-night shopping with her boyfriend in Brighton.

After a warm-up, we read through our lines, perfecting the dialogue that comes before the actual fight. '"I am for you"!' I say to Jake, pulling a paint brush out of the waistband of my trousers and holding it centimetres from his face.

'Oh, God! No! Don't *paint* me!' says Jake, cowering behind his hands.

'Use your imagination, Jake,' says Ms Kapoor. 'The prop knives will be here next week.'

'I still vote swords,' says Betty. She's standing next to Jake, clutching a bar of Galaxy instead of a knife.

'Betty,' says Miss, 'our play is set on an estate. How many sword fights take place on estates?'

'Loads?'

'No, not loads.' She starts to drag a block across the stage. 'Jake, help me with this.'

Betty and I jump off the stage and join Kat and Hoshi.

'You two ready for your "close-contact grapple"?' asks Kat, then she starts laughing.

'Miss shouldn't have called it that,' says Hoshi.

'*Grapple,*' says Betty, and Kat starts laughing all over again. '*Grapple, grapple, grapple!*'

I glance at my phone. I texted Mum to ask when she's getting home, but, as usual, she hasn't replied. Hoshi looks at me. 'You OK?'

'Could I come back to yours after rehearsal?' I say. 'I could sleep over.'

She pulls a face. 'Sorry. Dad's taking me to see a Japanese film. He's booked the tickets.'

'What about tomorrow?'

'We're going up to London to visit my uncle, but we'll be back in the evening –'

'Doesn't matter,' I say, dropping my phone back in my pocket.

'We've got the rehearsal on Sunday,' she says. 'I'll see you then.'

'I said it doesn't matter.'

'Betty, Pearl. Up on the stage,' calls Ms Kapoor.

Mr Simms has joined Ms Kapoor and Jake. 'As you know,' he says, 'I'm trained in t'ai chi.' He does a couple of deep lunges. 'I also have a qualification in dramatic combat, where I was taught to create the *illusion* of violence. Like this . . .' He turns round and swings a punch at Ms Kapoor, who throws herself back as if she's been hit on the shoulder.

'Kick him in the balls, Miss!' shouts Betty.

'No, she won't do that,' says Sir, 'because every act of violence is *choreographed*.'

They show us the fight they've planned for us and we watch, open-mouthed, as they roll around on the floor, pinning each other down and slapping each other about. 'Now I have seen everything,' whispers Betty as Ms Kapoor straddles Mr Simms and puts a ruler to his throat. Sir pushes her off and she does a backwards roll, landing by our feet.

She jumps up. 'Now it's your turn,' she says with a smile.

To begin with, it's just Betty and me fighting.

I pin Betty's arm behind her back. 'Does this remind you of when we were little?' she asks.

'Hold it and struggle,' calls Ms Kapoor.

'Do you remember when you gave me a nosebleed?' she asks as she tries to wriggle out of my grip. 'We were playing kiss-chase Power Rangers with Luke Miller.'

'Time for your first roll, Pearl,' says Miss.

Betty bends down and I flip forward over her shoulder. It looks like I'm falling, but actually Betty helps me go over. I laugh. 'You hit me on the nose because Luke was catching me more than you.'

'Concentrate, girls!'

'Sorry, Miss,' I say.

We practise our part of the fight several more times. 'And now,' says Ms Kapoor, 'Jake comes in. Romeo wants to stop the fight, so he's going to try and split you two up.'

'What do I do?' asks Jake, bouncing from foot to foot. He can't wait to get started.

'Pull Pearl off Betty.' As Ms Kapoor speaks she

demonstrates the move, grabbing me by my sleeve and yanking me back. 'Furious, Pearl then runs at you and knocks you to the floor.' She shoves Jake on the chest and he crumples dramatically to the ground. 'That's it. Then Pearl jumps on you and pins you down.'

'What?' I say.

'Sit on his chest,' she says.

'Really?'

'C'mon, Pearl,' says Jake, patting his blue T-shirt. 'Climb on board. I won't feel a thing. I'm steel.'

He's lying at the front of the stage and Kat and Hoshi are sitting on the floor just behind him, eyes wide. 'Like . . . *wow*!' says Kat, laughing. 'What are you waiting for Pearl?'

Jake grins. I fold my arms and glance at Hoshi. She smiles. 'OK,' I say. 'I can do this. It's a bit weird, but I can definitely do it.'

'Get up, Jake,' says Miss. 'I want Pearl to fly at you.'

He stands up and I walk to the back of the stage. 'Ready?' I ask.

'Ready.' He spreads his arms wide like he's in goal.

With a roar I run towards him, aiming for the red Levi logo in the middle of his T-shirt. My hands make contact and immediately he slams down on the floor and I jump on his chest, holding his wrists above his head. He pretends to struggle – he could knock me off easily if he wanted – but I keep his hands locked in place.

'Great!' says Miss. 'It looks perfect.'

'Can I get up now?' I ask. My face is centimetres away from Jake's. He smiles up at me, totally relaxed, as though this is the kind of thing we do every day.

'I guess we'll finish there,' says Miss. 'It's getting late.' As I go to get off Jake, he reaches up. 'What's that?' he asks, lifting my hair away from my face.

'That?' I jump up, touching the stinging edge of the bruise. 'I fell off a horse.'

'Let's see?' Hoshi has got on the stage and is next to Jake, peering at my face. 'When did you go horse riding?'

'Last night,' I pull my hair back over the bruise, 'when I got in.'

'You went horse riding in the dark?'

'I live at a stables, remember. There's an indoor school.' Jake and Hoshi both stare at me. 'Tonto's scared of water so Mum got me to do some work with him. Turns out he's really scared of water.' I know I'm babbling but I can't stop. 'This was caused by a puddle.'

'Were you unconscious?' asks Jake.

'Shut up! It's only a bump.' I feel my cheeks going red, so I turn away from them and get off the stage. 'I fell off a *standing* horse. It's my own fault. I wasn't wearing a helmet.'

Jake laughs. 'Well, it looks like a slice of pepperoni . . . As long as you know that.'

'Pepperoni?' I feel the bulging bruise again. Even though I touched it up before the rehearsal, some make-up must have come off.

'See you on Sunday,' says Jake with a wave.

Hoshi hangs around while I put on my shoes. 'My mum used to put white cabbage on a bruise and make me sleep with it there.'

'Didn't it fall off?' I check my phone one last time for messages.

'She made me wear a pair of tights on my head to keep it in place.' I look up from my phone, smiling. 'What?' she asks.

'Just a text from Mum. She'll be home soon.'

'Show her your head,' says Hoshi.

'So she can tie cabbage to it?'

She shrugs. 'I think you should show her. It looks bad.'

We follow the others out of the studio as Ms Kapoor turns off the lights.

'Promise you'll show her?' says Hoshi, putting her arm through mine.

'Maybe,' I say. 'C'mon. Let's catch up with the others.'

TWENTY-EIGHT

I open the back door and step into the warm kitchen. Mum's crumbling a stock cube into boiling water, pans are bubbling on the cooker and the windows are steamed up. '*Can you feel the love tonight, Pearl?*' she half sings. Show tunes blare out of the CD player. I glance at her hand. A glass of red wine is tilted dangerously to one side. 'Join in, Pearl! You used to be obsessed with *The Lion King*.'

I was. Jon took us to see the show in London and I loved it. 'What are you doing?' I ask, turning her music down.

'Making a roast!' she says, leaning over and turning it straight back up again.

'Really?' I peer in the oven. There's an enormous leg

of lamb inside and a tray of roast potatoes. 'Can we have Yorkshire puddings?'

She goes to the freezer and pulls out a box. 'Ta da! Top me up,' she says, passing me her glass. I fill it up with wine from the box on the table then hand it back to her. 'Peel the carrots, love.'

I sit down and start to peel. It reminds me of Sundays when Gran still lived with us. I'd watch her getting all the veggies ready and she'd tell me about the stuff she'd got up to when she was young, and even madder stories about Mum. My favourite was when Mum ran away to Morocco 'with a van full of hippies' when she was seventeen. I used to get Gran to tell me about that again and again.

Mum starts to sing 'Memory' from *Cats*. She's got a good voice and it's so cosy and warm in here that I really don't want to say anything about my head. But then I think of tomorrow, when I might walk into an empty house, not knowing where Alfie is or what sort of mood he's in. Over at the cooker, Mum starts to sway in time to the music. I want it to be like this all the time, but that's never going to happen if I don't tell her what Alfie did.

I nibble the end of a carrot. 'Mum,' I say. She's humming over the bubbling gravy. '*Mum!*'

'Have we got mint sauce?' she asks.

'Look what Alfie did.'

She keeps on stirring, then drops the spoon with a sigh and turns round. 'What?' I'm holding up my hair. She glances at my head then leans back against the worktop, arms folded. 'What were you fighting about?'

'Nothing,' I say. She laughs. '*Honestly*. He just threw the remote at me!'

She breathes slowly through her nose. 'Well, this is all ruined now!' She turns round and starts turning off switches, slamming pans to the side.

'What are you doing?' I turn the hobs back on, then try to work out which pan went where.

'I'm so fed up of this, Pearl.' She stares at me, her eyes wide. 'You two *never* stop arguing and I just wanted one nice meal together . . . Now I'm going to have to shout at him, and you know what he's like. He gets in my face and I can't control him like Mum could. He's so big now!'

Outside, we hear the whine of Alfie's bike. Then the engine cuts out.

'If I have a go at him,' she hisses, glancing at the door, 'you won't be the only one with a bruise!'

We stare at each other. 'Then don't say anything,' I say. '*Please, Mum.*' I grab her glass and fill it up again. I can hear Alfie's footsteps getting closer. 'We'll have a nice meal. We won't argue. I promise!'

She stays where she is, twirling the glass round in her hands, mouth squeezed shut. Alfie slams into the kitchen. 'Alright,' he says, looking at us and frowning. His eyes flick over my forehead. 'What's going on?'

Mum keeps twirling her glass.

'We're having a roast with Yorkshire puddings!' I say, then I start to gather all the stuff on the table into one pile. 'I'll do the knives and forks.'

After a moment, Alfie says, 'Can't we eat in the other room?'

I look at Mum and she nods. I leave the magazines,

letters and mugs where they are and pull out three trays instead. 'Smells amazing, Mum,' I say.

'Yeah, it does,' says Alfie. 'Best smell in the world.'

Mum smiles and turns up the CD player even louder. 'Circle of Life' fills the kitchen.

We eat our roast watching *Coronation Street*. Ozzie's nose is pressed on Mum's knee, her tail thumping. Every now and then she gets something to eat, which makes her tail wag even faster. 'Wait . . .' says Mum, dangling a bit of meat over her nose. Then she drops it and Ozzie snaps it up. 'Good girl!'

'Hey, Pearl,' says Alfie when the adverts come on. 'Remember Gran's cauliflower cheese that she did with roast beef?' Mum leans back on the sofa and looks at me.

'It was my favourite,' I say. 'I loved that crunchy topping.'

'Sorry I didn't make you any cauliflower cheese,' says Mum.

'It wouldn't go with lamb,' I say quickly.

'I'm going out tomorrow,' she says. *Coronation Street* has come back on and Alfie is frowning at the screen. 'I'm going with Heather to the races in Brighton. We're staying the night at her sister's.'

'Win some money for me, Mum,' says Alfie.

'I might. There's a horse running called Alfie's Luck.'

'Here's a tenner,' says Alfie, pulling a note out of his wallet. 'Do what you want with it and if you win anything you can keep it.'

'Thanks, sweetheart!' He puts his feet up on her lap and she gives his legs a stroke. They've been sitting like this since Alfie was little. 'Do you two promise me to be good?' she asks. 'No fighting?'

'Yes, Mum,' I say.

'No chucking stuff, Alfie,' she says, giving his knee a squeeze.

'Nope,' he says, then he curls up on his side and pulls a pillow under his head. Mum sips her wine and goes back to watching TV. After a couple of seconds, Alfie's eyes slide on to me.

I stare at the TV, but I know his eyes are fixed on my

face. My dinner sits heavily in my stomach. Eventually he turns back to look at the screen. 'Enjoy the races, Mum,' he says. 'Me and Pearl will be fine.'

She smiles and pats his feet.

TWENTY-NINE

The next day, I manage to avoid Alfie all day by going to work – Jane's let me swap my shifts round so I can go to the big rehearsal tomorrow. I stay as late as possible at World of Water, but eventually Jane says it's time to go and insists on dropping me at home.

I let myself into the dark house and immediately Ozzie dashes into the kitchen, skids on the lino and jumps up at my chest, patting me with her paws. She misses Mum. I let her out and she runs up and down the garden, barking at trees and hedges. 'Alfie?' I shout. There's no reply.

I take my work sweatshirt off and dump it in the washing machine. Then I go through to the living room and stand still. Everything is quiet upstairs. I walk through the silent house to my bedroom and grab some clothes off my bedroom floor.

Once I've got the washing machine going, I put on some music and check my fish. 'Hey,' I say. I follow them with my eyes as they dart around. 'Hello, Oy.' He's right at the front of the tank. 'You're being brave swimming with the big fish.' He shoots back to his pink coral like he's heard me. I need to clean them out, but first I need to clean me. I sniff my hands. I stink of work. Even though I washed my hands, I still smell of weed and fish and the dusty food I've been sprinkling into tanks all day.

I get a towel off the end of my bed and go upstairs.

I wait until the shower is boiling hot then tread carefully into the bath, standing on tiptoe to keep my feet away from the scuzzy crust of dried shampoo and shower gel. I shut my eyes and let the water run through my thick hair and thunder on my shoulders. I lift my face to the spray and wash off all my make-up, then I use handfuls of shower gel until I finally get rid of the fishy smell. Soon I'm padding downstairs wrapped up in a towel and smelling of pink grapefruit.

Then I see football playing on the T.V.

'Alright?' says Alfie, glancing up from the sofa. Water drips from my hair on the carpet. Ozzie's stares at me and her tail thumps on the floor. 'Mum's left us money to get pizza.'

'OK.' I tap the banister with my nails. 'Are you going out?'

'I can't be bothered,' he says. 'Too cold.'

I stand on the stairs. I've got to find something to do. I could text Tiann, but she'll be round at Max's. Kat's got family over. I wonder if Hoshi's back from London yet.

'Do you want a cup of tea?' says Alfie.

I look up. 'What?'

'*Tea.*' He speaks slowly like I'm an idiot. 'Do you want one?'

I'd love a cup of tea. I've been working for eight hours straight and Jane kept being called into the garden centre so I didn't get my breaks. 'Yes, please,' I say.

He gets up, pushing Ozzie out of the way with his foot. 'Two sugars?'

I nod. 'Thanks.'

He laughs. 'It's just a cup of tea.'

I pull my towel closer to me and go to my room. I get dressed, throwing on tracksuit bottoms and a hoodie. Maybe I don't need to go out tonight. I could sort my room out. I turn up my music and start to chuck all the dirty clothes in one pile. I put the plates and bowls by the door, trying not to look too closely at the furry mould that's growing on some rock-hard Cheerios.

There's a knock at the door and Alfie pops his head in, holding out a steaming mug of tea. 'Thanks,' I say, taking it. He grunts then disappears down the dark corridor. The mug's burning my fingers, so I put it down while I collect up all Mum's old *Chat* magazines. Headlines jump out at me: 'Potty Pets', 'Evil Scumbag', 'Mummy's Last Kiss' . . . I sit on my bed and arrange them into a stack. Somehow I find myself reading 'My Dentures Are Haunted'. Betty would love it.

I rip out the article then sip my tea. It's just right.

I wrap my hands round the mug and look out of the window. It's already dark and through the trees I can see the flickering lights of the stables. I take another sip of the sweet tea. Suddenly, something bumps against my lip. I pull the mug back, brown tea dripping over the magazine. I go to hook out the teabag, but it's not a teabag. It's something feathery and fringed with black.

I stare as an orange and white shape bobs to the surface of the hot tea. For a second my brain can't make sense of what I'm looking at, then I gasp and throw the mug on the floor and Oy bounces on to the carpet.

Immediately I'm down on my knees picking him up, one hand clutched to my mouth, and I know what Alfie has done. I left my door unlocked – just for five minutes – but it was all he needed. Sick rises into my throat as I stroke my finger along Oy's beautiful white stripes. I can't breathe properly. Hands shaking, I find a sock and put Oy on it. His mouth is gaping and his eyes are dull black dots.

Then I scream and I'm running down the corridor. Alfie's lying on the sofa laughing so hard his eyes are shut. I fly at him. 'I hate you,' I shout, thumping his chest. 'I *hate* you!'

I try so hard to hurt him, but he just holds my arms and pushes me away. 'What?' he says, still laughing. 'It's just a fish, Pearl!' So I go for him again, thrashing my head around, trying to get at him any way I can.

Then it's like a switch has flicked. Alfie's smile disappears and he throws me off him and bangs me down on the carpet, pinning my arms to my sides. He puts his face close to mine. 'I told you not to tell Mum,' he says slowly, his eyes wide. 'But you did!' The skin on my wrists is starting to burn, but he doesn't let go. 'You shouldn't have done that.'

He's breathing wildly, eyes not blinking. 'You *killed* him,' I say. He loosens his grip, so I try to pull my wrists free but he squeezes his fingers shut again.

'Don't mess with me, Pearl,' he says and he stares at me until I stop struggling. Finally he lets go of my wrists. 'You're blocking the TV,' he says, swinging his legs on to the coffee table. Ozzie has been pressed against the wall, but now she brushes past me and jumps up by Alfie.

I sit on the carpet and stare at the dog hairs that are

all over my tracksuit bottoms. 'I hate you,' I say. The room glows blue from the TV screen.

'Yeah, you said.'

Heart pounding, I get up and go to my room. I feel like it was my throat that he squeezed. I pick up the sock and put it on my pillow, then I pull on my trainers, grab my keys and lock my bedroom door. I walk past Alfie and out of the house, letting the door slam shut on the sound of a cheering crowd.

Head down, I walk down the track, gasping mouthfuls of the frosty air. My wet hair whips in my face and I hold my hoodie tight under my chin. As I head for the dual carriageway, a thin mist of rain starts to fall.

Cars and lorries fly past, their lights picking me out at the side of the road, but no one notices me. I pause at the top of the underpass, look down the slope at the puddles and the flickering yellow light. I turn away and walk towards the traffic.

I stand with my toes hanging off the pavement. The cars are so close I could touch them. I see a gap and I step out, walking across the road as horns blast and lights dazzle me. I keep going until I reach the grass in the middle. A passing lorry makes my body shudder. I wait, then, seeing my chance, I step over the barrier and out into the endless stream of traffic. I stare straight ahead and I walk, and I don't care what happens.

THIRTY

Hoshi's dad answers the door. 'Hello?' he says, staring at me.

'It's me.' I pull my hood down. 'Hoshi's friend.'

'Sorry. I didn't recognise you.' My hand automatically goes to the bump on my forehead, then I remember that I'm not wearing any make-up. I always wear make-up. 'Come in,' he says, standing back. 'Hoshi's in her room.'

I leave my trainers in the hall and go barefoot up the stairs, my feet leaving damp patches on the fake wood. I stand outside Hoshi's door, then I knock and go in. She's sitting cross-legged on her bed, wearing a spotty onesie. 'Hello!' she says, looking up. She smiles. 'What are you doing here?' I sit down next to her, flop back and stare at the ceiling. 'You look –'

'Like crap,' I say. 'I know. No make-up. Wet hair.'

'Like a pretty ghost,' she says. I turn and look at her, eyes narrowed. 'See.' She holds up the comic she's reading. 'You're like Chika.' She taps a drawing of a pale girl with huge eyes. 'She was killed on prom night and now she haunts the school, luring hot boys to their deaths.'

'It does sound like something I might do.'

'Your hands are blue. You're freezing.' She gets a blanket from the bottom of the futon and throws it over me.

'Thanks, Mum,' I say. 'What's this music?'

'It's songs from the Studio Ghibli films. They're Japanese cartoons. Do you like it?'

I listen to the sweeping piano music. 'No.'

Hoshi laughs. 'Have you ever seen a Ghibli film?' I shake my head. 'My favourite is *Princess Mononoke*.'

I curl up on my side and pull the blanket under my chin. '*Princess Mono-whaty?*'

'*Mononoke.*'

'Tell me about it,' I say.

She wriggles round to face me. 'There's this Emishi warrior, Ashitaka, and he gets involved in a fight between humans and nature gods.' She starts talking about wolf goddesses and monks, waving her hands around and occasionally slipping into Japanese. Soon I feel my eyes closing, lulled by the music and Hoshi's voice, and totally exhausted with being me.

For a moment, I don't know where I am, then I feel a prickly blanket and remember that I'm at Hoshi's. Oy is dead in my room. My lips drank that tea.

I sit up, my head muzzy. A Hello Kitty clock tells me it's nine. I've been asleep for nearly two hours!

I head towards the voices coming from the kitchen, but when I get to the door I don't know what to do.

'Pearl?' Hoshi calls. I push open the door and blink into the bright light. 'I'm making us Japanese food,' she says. 'You woke up just in time.'

She's standing at the cooker, still wearing her onesie, but with an apron over the top. Her dad is sitting at the table behind a laptop. 'Hello,' he says, glancing up.

He's holding a bottle of beer, drips of condensation running down the side of the green glass. 'Did you have a good rest?'

I nod and pull my sleeves over my hands. 'Sorry. I was tired from work.'

I've still got that lump in my throat and it's making talking hard.

'Come and sit over here,' says Hoshi, nodding at a stool. 'Ignore Dad. He looks like he's doing work, but he's actually building his Minecraft Godzilla.'

'I'm doing her teeth,' he says, not looking up from the screen. 'It's difficult.'

I watch as Hoshi chops spring onions into tiny circles. 'Can you stay the night?' she asks, turning back to the cooker and spreading an omelet out thin. She starts folding it over and over on itself until it makes a roll. 'We can go in to the rehearsal together in the morning.'

I lean on the counter, put my chin in my hand and look at Hoshi. She's wearing the kitten ears tonight, but they're almost hidden by her hair. She glances at me. 'OK,' I say. Rain drums against the black window but the kitchen is dazzlingly lit by rows of spotlights.

She grins. 'In a minute, we're going to watch *Princess Mononoke*.'

'A cartoon?'

'The *best* cartoon.'

I yawn. 'No way can it be better than *The Lion King*.'

All of a sudden, Hoshi's dad starts to sing 'Hakuna Matata', tapping his beer bottle on the table in time to imaginary music. His voice is surprisingly deep and he goes red when he notices us watching him.

'Dad!' Hoshi cries.

'I vote *Lion King*,' he says with a shrug.

Hoshi looks at me and I nod. 'Two against one,' she says. 'You win.'

We eat in front of the TV, plates balanced on our knees, a white Christmas tree twinkling away in the corner of the room.

It might be the best food I've ever tasted. I eat everything I'm given: strips of pepper fried in batter, cold noodle salad, rice with green beans and the rolled-up omelets – *tamagoyaki*. As 'The Circle of Life' crashes out and Scar dangles a mouse over his mouth, Hoshi uses her chopsticks to point at the food on my plate. '*Edamame*,' she says, '*daikon, katsuo*. It should be better, but Dad's a vegetarian and as it's his birthday I thought I'd only make things he could eat.'

'Why didn't you tell me?' I say, looking up and noticing the cards on the mantelpiece.

'But that's why it's so cool you turned up,' says Hoshi.

'*Shh*,' says her dad. 'I love this bit.' It's a shot of a misty plain, rain falling over distant mountains. 'It reminds me of Japan.'

Hoshi gets me seconds – it's like nothing can fill me up – then we eat this sweet pink squidgy stuff called *chi chi dango*. I dip a piece in my tea and suck off the icing sugar as Scar and Simba rip into each other.

Suddenly, I can't eat another thing, so I put the last bit of *chi chi* down on my plate and curl up on the futon. I watch *The Lion King*, my feet next to Hoshi's, my arms wrapped round a cushion, and in my head I sing along to every song.

I borrow one of Hoshi's T-shirts and she lets me have the best side of her futon. Then we lie in the dark, and she tells me about her life in Japan, about what it's like having a British dad and being a 'halfie'. She says that people think she's pretty because of her nose. 'People in Japan say it's *hana takai,* which means "high". I basically got into Baby Girlz because of my big nose.' She laughs.

'You've got a tiny nose,' I say.

'Not in Japan. It's massive there.' Then she talks about her mum. 'I miss her noodle omelet,' she says. 'And I miss her. It's the longest we've ever spent apart. The funny thing is, when I was at home I always wanted her to go away. You know, everything about her annoyed me. Even her voice.'

'I don't think I see enough of my mum for her to annoy me.' Hoshi's cartoon music is still playing in the background. 'Your dad is nice,' I say. 'Quiet.'

'I know. Some people think he's in a mood, but he just doesn't like talking. What's your dad like?'

'Fat.'

She laughs. 'What else?'

'I don't know. He might not be fat now. I hardly ever see him.' I explain that he lives in Liverpool with his new family. 'I used to visit with Alfie,' I say, 'but his wife gets on my nerves.' I roll on to my back and stare at the ceiling. Hoshi has left the curtains open and the street lights are shining in. 'She's got a tattoo of Elvis on her shoulder and wears wet-look leggings with bullet holes printed on them.'

'She sounds cool.'

'You wouldn't say that if you'd had to walk round Tesco with her.' A car goes past, lighting up the room. 'Actually, she's not that bad. She's nice to me.' For a second, we both fall quiet. Way off in town, a police siren wails.

Just when I think Hoshi might have fallen asleep, she says, 'What about your brother? What's he like?'

I nearly say 'an idiot' or 'a freak' because that's what

236

I always say, but the lump is coming back into my throat and I'm not sure I can speak. Outside, a car door slams and the Hello Kitty clock ticks out the seconds. 'Today he killed one of my fish,' I say. 'He killed Oy.'

'*What?*'

'And he throws stuff. Hits me.' It's the first time I've ever said these words out loud. Except to Mum.

'He can't do that!' She's sitting up, looking at me.

'I hit him back . . . Well, I used to.' I say.

'Everyone hits their brothers and sisters when they're little,' says Hoshi, 'but not when they're, what, seventeen?'

'How do you know?' I say, my voice hard.

'You should tell your mum.'

I laugh. 'Mum knows.' I roll to face her and pull the duvet up round my shoulders. 'She says I've got to stop winding him up.'

We stay like that for a moment. 'It'll be OK, Pearl,' Hoshi says and she puts her hand on my shoulder.

I stare at her. What does she know, with her dad who just drinks two beers then has a cup of tea, and her shiny laminate floor and her three bank cards crammed into her panda purse? Hoshi can't even begin to understand why this will *never* be OK. 'I'm tired,' I say and I shut my eyes, but I know she's still staring at me so I turn my back on her. Soon I hear her lie back down.

'I could help you,' she says. 'The girls too. Have you told them?' I shake my head. 'I know you can sort this out. You're a strong person. It's one of the things I first noticed about you when I saw you standing up on the stage.'

'Alfie's stronger,' I mutter.

'I don't believe it,' she says.

I pull the duvet up higher. 'You've never met him.' I lie still and silent until eventually I hear her breathing getting deeper.

But I can't sleep. My heart is racing and my mind won't calm down. More than anything I wish I could take back what I just told Hoshi and hide it away again. I press my face into the pillow, squeeze my eyes shut and wait until the sick feeling inside me starts to fade.

THIRTY-ONE

Ms Kapoor hands me a white bin bag. 'TYBALT' is written on the side in thick marker pen. 'I think you'll like it,' she says. 'It's mainly black.'

All around me, students are pulling their costumes out, squealing and holding up vests and dresses to show friends. I tip out a pair of ripped black jeans and a white T-shirt with a leopard's face covering half of it. A pair of hoop earrings and a leather jacket land on top.

'You'll need to wear boots or trainers,' says Miss. I pick up the jeans and put my fingers in the rips. It looks like the leopard has run its claws through them. 'OK, Pearl?' I look up. I've been in a daze all morning and Hoshi practically had to drag me to school. 'You look pale.'

'It's just that I used Hoshi's make-up,' I say. 'She's into the natural look.'

'I like it.'

'I don't,' I say, touching my eyebrows. Today everyone can see how pale my eyebrows and eyelashes are.

'What do you think of your costume?' she asks. I feel the soft leather of the jacket. 'I used to wear that at college.'

'Good,' I say.

'Miss!' Betty appears in the studio wearing a baggy khaki shirt over a tight vest and denim cut offs. 'I love it. I look badass!'

'Have you made those shorts shorter?' Ms Kapoor starts to examine the turn-ups.

'Don't touch them,' says Betty, running away. 'Mercutio would definitely have been into hot pants.'

All the Montagues' clothes are vaguely military, while the Capulets are going to wear black. The exception is Hoshi.

'Do you like it?' she asks me. She's holding up a white

240

skater dress and swishing it from side to side. The dress has tiny holes cut all over it and a fitted bodice.

I shrug. 'It matches your hair.'

'Seriously, Miss?' says Kat, staring at a khaki shirt. 'There's nothing else in our bags.' Bea's also got one of the shirts and is trying it on over her top.

'I ran out of money,' says Ms Kapoor.

'Buying cool clothes for everyone else!' Kat holds the shirt at arm's length, like it's contaminated. 'Please tell me I can pimp this shirt,' she says, looking at Hoshi's dress through narrowed eyes. 'So unfair . . .'

'Right.' Ms Kapoor raises her voice. 'Everyone get changed. I need to see what you look like and if everything fits.'

'It would fit my dad,' mutters Kat as we head for the toilets.

After we've wandered around in our costumes and Ms Kapoor has checked us over, we change back into our normal clothes and start to rehearse. We do most of the show, skipping the odd scene that we haven't fully prepared. We stop and start and at one point we spend half an hour perfecting three minutes of a song. With just over a week of rehearsals left, we're all aware that we've not got long to sort out any problems.

Very quickly, the mucking around and laughing stops and the crying begins. It always happens just before a show. Evie cries because Betty elbows her in the boob during a dance; Bus Kelly cries because her cat died three weeks ago; and Kat cries because Miss says she's going to need her to 'stop doing that weird thing with her lips'.

By the end of the rehearsal, we still haven't managed to get the opening dance right and I think Ms Kapoor might cry. Instead she goes with screaming.

We all stand and watch her as she crouches down, puts her head in her hands and screams quietly into her knees. Mr Simms stops playing the piano.

'Is she actually pulling her hair out?' Jake whispers in my ear.

'I think she's acting,' I say.

She stays curled up for a moment longer, then looks up. 'That's it for today,' she says with a mad smile.

'Good idea,' says Mr Simms. 'Remember, it's Juliet, the nurse and her parents rehearsing after school tomorrow.' He goes to help Ms Kapoor to her feet and we all drift out of the studio.

After saying goodbye to the girls, Hoshi and I walk across the playing field.

'Do you want to stay at mine?' she asks.

'No. I'm fine,' I say. All through the rehearsal she's been glancing at me anxiously and I've been regretting what I said last night.

'Or I could come back with you to your place.'

I laugh. 'No way.' I don't want Hoshi sitting on our stained sofa in the dark living room, her feet finding a space on the carpet between the abandoned mugs and ash trays.

'I could tell your mum what Alfie's been doing, about your fish. How Alfie hit you the other day, because that is what happened, isn't it?'

'Oh my God, Hoshi,' I say, walking a bit faster. 'I told you Mum doesn't care. And no, he didn't hit me. He threw a remote control at me.'

Hoshi grabs my arm. 'You can't go home, Pearl. You need to do something!'

'There's nothing I can do,' I say, pulling away from her and walking on.

'There must be . . . You could tell Ms Kapoor. You could call the police!'

This makes me laugh. '*Hello? Is that the police?*' I say, speaking into an imaginary phone. '*My brother and I had a fight and he was mean to me . . . You'll send someone to arrest him? Cheers!*'

'Hey!' she says, catching up with me. 'You can make jokes, but whatever Alfie is doing, you can't keep ignoring it!'

I stop walking and face her. 'Why not?' I say, my voice rising. 'Because that's what I've always done and I'm alright, aren't I?'

We stand in the muddy field, staring at each other. Hoshi's wearing her Montague Santa hat and her face is lit up by the setting sun. After everything I did to her when she arrived, this is what's finally wiped the sunny smile off her face.

'Look, I'll be fine,' I say. 'When Alfie does something like this he feels bad. He'll leave me alone for ages now.' A shout across the dark field makes us turn round. Jake's running towards us.

I know Hoshi wants to say something, but she can't because Jake has caught up with us. I step to one side so he can walk between us. 'How mad was Ms Kapoor?' says Jake, throwing his arms round us, drawing us closer.

'She didn't like it when you asked for a tighter vest,' I say.

'The audience deserve to see my ripped chest. It's what they're paying for . . . So what were you two talking about?'

'Your ripped chest,' I say.

'Thought so!' he says, then we walk across the field together and I laugh extra loud at everything Jake says.

He stays with us all the way to Hoshi's road. He says his dad lives round the corner, but I'm not so sure. We stand on the pavement, talking about the show, until I realise Jake's not going anywhere. In fact, I think he's waiting for me to go away.

'So I'll see you tomorrow?' I say.

'Do you want to come in for a bit?' asks Hoshi. 'We could watch *Princess Mononoke*.'

'No, thanks.' I start to walk down the road. 'I need to get home.'

'See you at band call!' calls Jake, then he says in a quieter voice to Hoshi. 'I can come to yours. We could practise the balcony scene. We keep getting it wrong.'

I don't hear Hoshi's reply. I just walk away, heading for the underpass, and soon I'm crunching through the dead leaves on the track that leads to the farm.

Just as I'm walking past the field, a shape looms out of the darkness. I stop walking. 'Hello, Tonto,' I say. He stares at me, just out of reach. I put my hand out to him and this time he lowers his head and sniffs. He takes a step closer, then another. 'Do you remember me?' I ask.

With one more step he's reached the fence and he's towering over me. Automatically I find myself standing taller. Mum drummed it into me that I had to 'stand like a queen' whenever I was around the horses, 'shoulders back, chest out'. I put my cheek against his warm face and he leans in to me and breathes into my hair. Behind him, I can see our house. There's a light on in the kitchen. 'I've got to go,' I say, but I don't move. Instead I wrap my arms round his neck and just hold on until he shakes me away.

It's Mum I find in the kitchen, reading the paper, her hand round a mug of coffee. She doesn't look up. 'Hello, love,' she says.

My shoulders relax and I'm so relieved I shut my eyes for a second. 'Hi, Mum,' I say, then I walk through the dark living room to my bedroom.

Oy is still lying on the sock on my pillow, only now he's dry and his eyes have sunk into his head. His bright orange stripes have faded. I sit on my bed and hold him on my lap, surrounded by mess. I don't even bother turning the tank light on. The lump that's been in my throat since Saturday gets bigger until I start to worry that I can't breathe. I take deep breaths and wonder if I'm having a panic attack. Evie's always having them. I thought she was faking them, but now I'm not so sure.

247

'What's wrong?' Mum's standing in the doorway holding her coffee. Ozzie peeks round her legs. 'Why are you making those noises?'

'Can't breathe,' I say, then I hold up the sock. 'Oy's dead.'

Mum sighs. 'They're always dying, Pearl. You know that. When you spend money on those fish you're flushing it down the toilet. Literally.' She comes further into the room and sits on the end of the bed. 'He was your favourite, wasn't he?' I nod. 'I remember when Jon bought him for you and told you to call him Oyster.'

'So I'd never forget how precious pearls are,' I say numbly.

'That's right.' Mum puts her hand on my back for a moment then takes it away. She waves a finger at Oy. 'Shall I get rid of it for you?'

I shake my head and watch as Ozzie goes to my bubbling fish tank and puts her nose against the glass. Her eyes flick left and then right as she watches the fish. I put my shoulders back, sit up a bit taller. 'Alfie killed him,' I say.

Mum laughs. 'Of course he did.' She gets up quickly and a splash of coffee lands on her dirty jodhpurs.

'But, Mum –'

'Not now, Pearl.' She rubs at the stain with her sleeve. 'I don't want to hear another word. When was the last time you asked how my day went? If I had a good time in Brighton?' I turn away from her and look out of the window. Everything inside me feels heavy. 'We used to go riding together!' She says this like she's amazed it ever happened. She takes the sock off my lap and walks out of my room, shouting, 'Ozzie!' over her shoulder. Ozzie's ears stand up, then she bounces after her.

I lie down on my side. Mum's right. Fish do die all the time and Oy was probably eight. That's old for a clown fish in captivity. In the ocean he might have lived up to fifty years.

My tank is still alive with beautiful fish, but there was only one Oy.

I feel like I'm stuck to the bed, stuck to this house. A month ago, dreams of being Juliet and performing with Jake lifted me up and away from here. What have I got

249

now? I'm all on my own and, for all I know, Jake is round at Hoshi's, up in her room, practising their lines.

I get out my phone. **Good night, good night . . .** I text. Then I stare at the screen. Almost immediately Hoshi replies: **Parting is such sweet sorrow! Attai.**

It's funny how a few words can make you feel so much better.

THIRTY-TWO

The show and Christmas arrive at the same time.

When I get home from school on Monday, our box of Christmas decorations is sitting on the kitchen table and that evening we all eat pasta together watching a Simpsons Christmas special. Dad's sent Alfie an early present – a set of golf clubs – so he's in a good mood and there's no fighting. Mum smiles and says she's going to go up into the attic to find the Christmas tree, but then she falls asleep. Alfie and I don't care enough about a tree to wake her up.

It's true what I told Hoshi: Alfie leaves me alone all week. He barely looks at me the couple of times we pass each other at home. School becomes this strange mix of skivy lessons – because it's the last week of term – and intense rehearsals. We break up on Friday, but we hardly notice because everyone in the cast stays in school late, perfecting the finale.

Alfie and I avoid each other all weekend and then I'm waking up on Monday morning, slightly amazed that it's just two days until opening night. We're doing the technical at the theatre today and I'm so excited that I jump out of bed and rush to get ready. I manage to slip out of the house before anyone else is up.

The sun's still rising as I walk past the frost-covered fields and everything glows in the pink light. I can't help smiling: I'm walking away from home, we're two days away from opening night and I'm going to the theatre, my favourite place in the world.

Jake and Hoshi's profiles are on posters all over town. '*Romeo and Juliet: the Musical*,' they say. 'Get ready to fall in love . . .' I meet Hoshi standing next to the poster outside WHSmith. When she sees me, she poses for a moment just like her photo, face turned to one side, eyes wide open, a smile playing on her lips. Then she turns and grins. 'I'm so excited!' she says.

'Me too.'

'Everything OK?' she asks, putting her arm through mine.

'*Yes!*' Hoshi's been asking me this all week. 'By the way,' I say, 'I'm ignoring your hat.'

She tugs on one of the long grey ears flopping down over her eyes. 'He's Totoro. A sort of rabbit spirit. Pretty cool.'

'You're wearing a rabbit on your head.'

'Exactly!' she says.

We walk on past the town Christmas tree and shops covered in sale posters, our breath misting the air and our cheeks turning pink. Soon we get to the theatre. 'Here we are,' I say and together we look across the road. The theatre is modern with big windows reflecting the blue sky. '*ROMEO AND JULIET* 16th–18th December' is written on a banner that hangs across the whole building.

'This feels way too real,' says Hoshi.

'I like thinking it is real,' I say, still staring at the banner, 'and that this is my job and I get to do it every day.'

'I feel sick,' she mutters.

'Hoshi! This theatre seats seven hundred people. You've performed in *stadiums*.'

'This is different,' she says. 'Scarier. I was one of a crowd then.' Her phone rings in her bag. She glances at the number and sends it to answerphone.

'Who was that?'

'My agent,' she says, as we cross the road. 'She won't stop ringing me.'

'Why?' Something about the casual way she says this worries me.

'A new band is forming,' Hoshi replies, walking ahead of me into the theatre. 'Would you believe they want me in it?'

'What?' I stop walking.

She looks back at me. 'I'm not doing it.'

'But you could see your mum.'

'Mum's had me for years. It's Dad's turn.'

'You'd be famous again.'

'And have to smile, and giggle, and pretend to be happy all the time? No way! There are too many good things about living here.' She pulls me after her. 'Come on.'

Together we cross the empty foyer. Blue carpet stretches to the shuttered kiosks, where boxes of sweets are arranged in rows.

I push open double doors and then we're standing at the back of the auditorium. Rows of empty seats lead to the vast stage, that's lit with a bright light. The set is up: a graffitied wall covered in ivy and a silhouetted skyline of a city. Juliet's balcony is there too: a normal railing on a block of flats with a flower box filled with trailing red flowers. Somewhere backstage we can hear voices. 'It looks like a fairytale,' I say. 'If you ignore all the litter.'

Hoshi nods and starts to walk down the aisle, tilting her head back and turning round to look at the ceiling covered in tiny lights. 'It's even got a sky,' she says.

My fingers trail over the backs of seats as I walk towards the stage. The carpet is soft under my feet and it's so quiet. 'It feels like something is about to happen,' I say.

'It is,' says Hoshi, and together we go up the curving steps and on to the stage.

Just like every other show I've done, the technical is bad. We forget our entrances, trip over props and bang into each other during the dances, but we know it's getting there. Chris is our stage manager and he keeps us organised. At the end, he says he's 'not panicking . . . yet', which I think is a good thing.

Afterwards, we go back to our dressing rooms. Ours is tucked away at the top of the theatre and although it's meant for two, all five of us are squeezed in the tiny room. This just makes it more fun. Kat's brought her iPod speakers and Betty puts up a picture of Leonardo DiCaprio from an old film of *Romeo and Juliet* 'for inspiration'. Already, make-up and clothes are everywhere.

Ms Kapoor sticks her head in the door. 'Tidy up in here before you go,' she says, 'and set your alarms tonight: I don't want anyone to be late tomorrow. We're going to need every minute of our dress rehearsal time.'

'Yours,' says Betty, throwing a hoodie in my direction. I catch it and when I look up Hoshi is staring intently at her phone. Our eyes meet.

'Still not interested,' she says with a smile. Betty passes her the Totoro hat and she pulls it on.

'Really?' I say. I try to imagine what it must feel like to turn down a chance like that, how bad it must have been last time to want to stay in this boring town with us.

'*Really*,' she says.

THIRTY-THREE

The next morning I'm awake before the alarm goes off and then I'm up and getting ready for a whole day at the theatre. Before I leave the house, I raid the fridge, and that's when I see the note: 'Gone to see a horse in Dorset. Back late. x Mum'

My first thought is that she's forgotten about the show tomorrow – her ticket is still sitting on the mantel-piece – then Alfie walks in and I realise that we'll be all alone tonight.

'Mum's getting back late,' I say quickly.

He pushes past me and grabs the milk. I go to shut the fridge, but his arm is in the way. He looks at me. 'Did you tell her I killed that fish?' he says.

'What?' My mouth goes dry and I step back. He

unscrews the milk and gulps some down, never taking his eyes off me. We both know I told her, but at exactly the same time as I'm thinking, *Why shouldn't I tell her*? I find myself saying, 'She saw me with it. I didn't say anything about you.'

'Really.' He slams the fridge door shut and something falls over. 'I told you not to say anything, Pearl . . .'

'I didn't,' I say, then I pick up my bag and walk straight out of the house. I go through the farm, fighting the urge to turn round and see if he's watching me out of the kitchen window. I feel like he is, and that's all it takes to make my heart beat faster.

As soon as we get to the theatre we run through scenes and dances that went wrong yesterday, then we get ready for the dress rehearsal. We do our hair and make-up, tape our mics in place and have a sound check on the stage. Then it's back to our dressing room to get into our costumes.

'What do you think?' asks Kat, rolling up the sleeves on her khaki shirt.

'I think you trod on me,' says Bea. She's trying to do the laces up on her boots. 'How've you done that?' She investigates Kat's shirt. 'We're wearing the same costume, so how come you look like a curvy lady, but I look like a chubby boy!'

'I got Mum to take it in,' says Kat, checking herself out in the mirror.

Bea stares down at her baggy shirt. 'Can she do mine tonight?'

'No way! Standing next to you is making me look even better.'

Bea shoves Kat, who bangs into Betty, who's putting on more eyeliner. 'Damn,' she says. 'Now I've got a tash.' Bea rubs at Betty's lip with the end of her shirt. 'Did you lick that?' asks Betty.

'Um . . . maybe.' Bea frowns. 'And I've made you look like Hitler.'

Hoshi and I got changed first and we watch all this from the battered armchair in the corner of the room. Hoshi's sitting on the arm and I've got the seat. Usually I'd be pumped right now, a few minutes away from the dress rehearsal, but I'm hardly thinking about the show. I wish Mum hadn't gone away. I feel sick whenever I think about going home tonight.

'Nervous?' says Hoshi.

I blink and look up at her. I shift my made-up face away from her white dress. 'Not at all,' I say. 'It's going to be amazing.'

'It is, isn't it? But you don't look very excited.'

'Just thinking about something.'

'What?' In the corner of the room, the speaker comes on and we can hear the orchestra tuning up.

'Nothing.' I put my little finger through one of the tiny holes in Hoshi's skirt. I'm wearing black sparkly nail varnish and I've filed my nails so that they're curving points.

Hoshi touches the end of one of them. 'Like a witch,' she says.

Across the room, Kat has managed to get the seat in front of the mirror and is doing her lipstick, her mouth wide open. She sees me looking at her and winks.

'Hoshi,' I say. 'Can I stay at your place tonight?'

'I said you can stay whenever you like.'

'But I've not got any of my stuff.'

'So get it after the rehearsal.'

'Maybe.'

The door opens and Ms Kapoor sticks her head in. 'All ready, girls?' Her eyes flick over each of us in turn. 'Kat, less boobs please.' Kat pulls a face and does up a button on her shirt. 'One more . . . and another one. Perfect. Ready to go in five minutes?'

We nod, suddenly quiet, and she moves on to the next dressing room.

I heave myself out of the squishy armchair and feel a bit of the mic wire come unstuck. 'Can you sort me out, Hoshi?' She rips off a piece of flesh-coloured tape with her teeth and smooths the wire back into place.

'Put on loads,' I say. 'I don't like it wriggling around.'

'I could come back to your place with you,' she says. Her fingers are cold on my back.

A voice comes through the speaker. 'Ladies and gentlemen, this is your five minute call.' I know it's Chris, but I can hardly recognise his voice.

'OK,' I say. 'We'll just go in and I'll grab my stuff . . . Thanks.'

'No worries.'

I pull my T-shirt down and take one last look in the mirror. I look tall and dangerous with my heavy eye make-up, pale lips and wild tangled hair. Next to me, Hoshi is a moth, her white dress swirling with every move she makes. I use one of my sharp nails to move a speck of mascara off my cheek. Now my face is smooth and blank.

'*Hana no youni kirei*,' says Hoshi.

I frown. 'I know that,' I say. I think back to when she used those words, weeks ago, on the bus. 'Are you saying I look like a carp's butt?'

She laughs. 'That's not what it really means. I said, "You're as beautiful as a flower."'

I smile. 'You punked me.'

'I've punked you loads,' she says.

'C'mon, you two,' says Kat from the door. 'Show time!'

★

The best thing that can be said about the dress rehearsal is that we get through it. Afterwards, we get changed, then sit in the auditorium waiting for Ms Kapoor's notes.

We're in the second row, our feet up on the seats in front, passing a bag of Butterkist between us. Ms Kapoor silences us all with a grim look. 'Let's start where it began to go wrong,' she says, 'in the opening scene. Evie, people don't generally giggle when they're fighting, and no improvised karate please . . .'

It takes half an hour for her to go through the whole play. The only comment directed at me is that I've lost my sparkle. Miss says, 'Find it before tomorrow evening, Pearl.'

She pauses and folds the sheet of paper she's holding. 'We'll finish with a general note about lines,' she says. 'Chris gave eight prompts. That was eight prompts too many. Hoshi and Jake, you may have the most lines, but that's not an excuse.' Next to me, Hoshi sinks lower in her seat. 'Get the balcony scene sorted.'

Kat quietly tuts Hoshi, who's hiding behind her

hands. Then Ms Kapoor breaks into a huge smile. 'But except for that, it was wonderful! Get a good night's sleep and be back here by six tomorrow.'

Kat jumps up and starts climbing over our knees. 'Sorry,' she says as her bag hits Bea's face. 'Leo's Skyping me in ten minutes. I've got to get home.' She pauses as she goes past me to squeeze my cheek. 'So excited! He's coming to watch the show on Saturday.'

She walks up the aisle. 'Kat,' I call after her.

She turns. 'I know: tell him to bring some Lakrisal.'

'They're Swedish sweets,' I tell Hoshi. 'I'm addicted to them and Leo is my supplier. Try one.' I search in my bag until I find the foil-covered packet. She takes one of the grey sweets. 'It's salty licorice.'

She puts one in her mouth. 'Intense,' she says, her eyes going wide. 'A bit like wasabi candy.'

'Hey.' Betty leans round Bea. 'You two want to come to McDonalds with us? We're meeting Ollie and Bill there for Quality Street McFlurries. Hoshi, you can finally set eyes on the hottest boy on the planet.'

'That'll be Ollie,' says Bea.

'Er, hardly,' says Betty. 'Ollie looks weirdly like an otter.'

'Says the girl dating the *sheep*.'

'I'd love to come,' says Hoshi, 'but I'm going round to Pearl's.'

'You are?' says Betty, blinking. 'No one *ever* goes round to Pearl's house. She forbids it.'

'Well, I'm in!' Hoshi makes it sound like it's the best invitation in the world, when actually it's the very worst. 'Come on, Pearl.' She pulls me out of my seat.

'Find out if she sleeps in a coffin!' Betty calls after us.

THIRTY-FOUR

Soon we're walking next to the dual carriageway and Hoshi's laughing hysterically every time a lorry goes past. She says the traffic's giving her 'mad energy', but once we're on the track to the farm, she falls quiet. 'It's so dark,' she says as we walk past the cows.

'No street lamps,' I say. The last traces of sunlight have disappeared and the only light comes from the low moon. 'Your eyes will adjust in a second.'

A shape darts in front of us. 'Whoa!' Hoshi waves her hands in front of her face. 'What was that?'

'A bat,' I say, laughing. 'Here it comes again.'

It's been months since I walked home with anyone. Tiann used to come back after school, but she stopped after she saw Alfie kick a hole in a wall. He discovered

Ozzie had chewed up his phone and he really lost it. Since then we've always gone back to hers. She says my place gives her the creeps.

We cross the farm and go into our garden. 'Watch out for bike parts,' I say, stepping round a rusty exhaust. 'Alfie uses this as a garage.'

We go into the kitchen. 'Hi, Alfie,' I call. 'I'm home.'

Silence. 'No one's in,' says Hoshi. I can tell she's relieved.

I shrug and whisper, 'Sometimes he's quiet.'

Then I turn on the kitchen light and it's like I'm seeing my home for the first time: the torn lino, a bare lightbulb hanging from the ceiling, missing cupboard doors. 'I hate washing up,' I say, waving my hand at the sink, as though the piles of bowls and plates are the only problem.

'Me too,' says Hoshi. 'It drives Dad mad.'

'C'mon.' I lead her through the sitting room, my eyes flicking up the stairs and over to the sofa, looking for Alfie. There's no sign of him. I get my key out and Hoshi waits as I unlock my bedroom door.

Without switching on the overhead light, I go to my tank, turn on the light and then I put on my music.

'*Beautiful* . . .' Hoshi walks straight to the tank and kneels down, fingers spread wide, her eyelashes almost touching the glass. 'You did all this?'

I start poking through the stuff on the floor, grabbing clothes and stuffing them in a bag. 'Most of it. You can feed them if you like. One pinch of the food in the blue pot.' I feel under the bed, looking for a missing boot.

'They've gone crazy!' she says, laughing. 'What's this one? It's got a stripy eye.'

'Butterfly fish.'

'This one's cool.' I look over and see Hoshi's finger following a dottyback as it slithers around the tank. 'It looks like it's been dipped in paint.'

'Pretty, isn't it?'

'So pretty . . . but kind of incredible too,' she says. Her face is reflecting the blue of the tank. 'It looks like it comes from another planet.'

'It's a bicolour *Pseudochromis* and it's meaner than it looks. It fights fish three times its size.'

She stands up and takes a step back from the tank. 'I've never seen anything like it, not in someone's house.'

'Ever seen anything like this?' I say, flicking on the light.

She looks around my room, takes in the clothes on my bed, my bare mattress, the painting of a cottage left over from when this was a dining room. 'You're not very tidy,' she says.

'It's horrible.' I kick a pile of clothes.

'Well, I like it.' She goes and picks up a photo from my chest of drawers. 'Who's this?'

'Me and Betty, on our first day of school.' We're wearing green checked dresses that reach halfway down our legs and bright white socks. The photo's been sitting there for years.

'You look like mini versions of you,' she says. Then she peers at a photo I've Sellotaped to the wall. It's of me and Kat this summer in Sweden. 'Wow . . . You look happy.'

In the photo, Kat and I are standing next to our kayak in our bikinis. I'm wearing a cap pulled low on my head. My face is in shadow, but you can still see my smile. 'I was,' I say. Then I pull out the necklace I'm wearing. 'Look, Kat's auntie made me this.' It's a silver pendant of half a kayak. 'Kat's got one too. They fit together.' Talking about Sweden immediately brings back the fading memories of our holiday: the tight feeling of salt water on my skin, the smell of suntan lotion, lying on sunbaked rocks and knowing I was hundreds of miles away from home.

'And what's this?' asks Hoshi, going to the window and picking up a glass rabbit that used to belong to Gran. She holds it up to the light. 'There's a rainbow inside it!'

'It's Murano glass. My granddad brought that back from Venice.' I lower my voice. 'It's the only nice thing Alfie hasn't broken. That's why it's in here. I'm protecting it.'

'Has he always broken stuff?' she asks, putting the rabbit back in its place.

'Always,' I say. 'Mum says it's a temper thing. She thinks it's got worse because he misses Gran. She looked after him loads when he was little.' I hear a creak in the corridor and glance at the open door. 'I'll get my tooth-brush so we can get out of here.'

I leave Hoshi studying my riding rosettes and old pictures of Tonto and go upstairs to the bathroom.

As I'm on my way back down, the back door slams and Alfie walks into the sitting room, dragging his golf bag behind him.

He sees me standing there then picks up the bag and tips it out on to the sofa. Clubs and balls tumble out, and one ball rolls down the corridor towards my bedroom. I watch Hoshi step into the corridor and stop the ball with her foot. She leans against the wall and smiles at me, one finger to her lips.

'I'm staying at a friend's tonight,' I say. Alfie picks up a driver and starts waving it around like it's a sword. He even adds sound effects to make it sound like it's swooshing through the air. He's obviously ignoring me, so I go down the last few stairs.

Just as I reach the bottom step, he jumps forward and blocks my way with the golf club. 'Look,' he says. 'I've just bought this off Callum.'

'Nice, but I've got to go.' I try to push the club out of the way but he's holding it in a tight grip.

'Say the password,' he says, a smile playing on his lips.

'Stop mucking around, Alfie. I've got to go.'

He stares at me and keeps the club locked in place. Knowing Hoshi is watching makes me see how ridiculous Alfie is. I wonder if I've exaggerated everything, turned him into some monster when he's just an annoying brother. But then he steps closer. 'I'm not mucking around,' he says. 'Why do you think I'm mucking around?'

Before I can think what to do, Hoshi walks into the room. 'Come on, Pearl,' she says. 'We need to get to mine.'

Alfie spins round, and when he sees her his cheeks flush red. He takes in Hoshi's pink trainers and puffy silver coat, his eyes settling on the two knots of hair on each side of her head. He lets the golf club drop away. 'Who are you?'

'A friend of Pearl's.'

He laughs. 'You're Pearl's friend?' The way he says this, smiling but serious at the same time, tells me he's in a dangerous mood. I try to catch Hoshi's eye: I need to get her to be quiet before he loses it. But she's not taking her eyes off him.

'Yeah, I'm her friend,' she says. 'What's funny about that?'

'Nothing . . . just Pearl's not got many friends.' He swings the golf club in a full circle, back in control, smiling. 'Most people round here know she's a skank . . . Don't they, Pearl?'

My heart's pounding. I know I should speak, but instead I stay where I am at the edge of the room and just watch as Hoshi steps closer to him, chin raised high. 'You shouldn't say that about her,' she says.

'Why not?' He grins. 'It's true! Ask anyone. They'll all tell you what Pearl's like.'

'Come on, Hoshi,' I say quickly. 'Alfie's winding you up. Let's go.' I push past Alfie, who has started putting a ball backwards and forwards against the wall.

'See you later, skank,' he says.

'Hey!' Hoshi's eyes are blazing. Alfie doesn't look up. 'I *said* you shouldn't say that about her!'

I see him smile behind his curly hair, but it's not real: his fingers are gripping the club so tight they've gone white. Slowly he looks up. 'Why don't you,' he says, leaning towards her, '*shut up.*'

I feel like all the air has gone from the room. Every noise – the buzz of the fridge in the kitchen, the club brushing the carpet – is amplified. My heart is beating so hard it almost hurts. 'Don't speak to her like that,' I manage to say.

'What?' he says. '*Her?*' He lifts up the golf club and prods Hoshi's shoulder with it. '*She* needs to get out of here.'

Suddenly I'm filled with rage. How dare he say this to her? How dare he touch her? My hand flies out, grabbing the end of the club. 'Leave her alone!' I say, my voice is loud now. 'I mean it!' I shove the club back towards him and stand between them.

He shakes his head. 'You don't tell me what to do, Pearl.'

I take a deep breath, then another, and I force myself to look right at him. I know what I have to say, but I feel sick inside. Then I remember Hoshi is behind me and I stand tall and put my shoulders back. 'Alfie, I want you to leave me alone.'

He stares at me, an incredulous smile spreading across his face. 'Oh my God,' he says. 'What're you talking about?'

'I'm talking about this,' I say, holding up my hair and showing him the bruise on my forehead. 'And the staple you put in my finger when I was five, and my fish that you killed, and "skank" and "cow", and every single thing you've thrown at me –' I'm shouting now – 'and the way you look at me like that!' I point at his sneering face. 'You have to stop!'

It's just me and him now, our eyes locked on to each other.

'What if I say it's not going to stop?' he says quietly.

'Then . . .'

'Yes?'

'I'll tell Mum everything.'

'Yeah? Good luck with that.'

276

'And I'll keep telling her until she listens and *nothing* is going to stop me.'

Alfie stares at me, eyes wide, his chest rising and falling. 'Yeah?' he says. Then, in a single, swift movement, he swings the golf club over my head and slams it into a picture on the wall. I put my hands up to my face as fragments of glass shower over me. 'Still going to tell her?' he asks.

I look up at him, shaking the glass off my hair. 'I'm not scared of you,' I say, amazed, reaching out to Hoshi. Her fingers wrap round mine, warm and strong. Alfie's eyes narrow and he pulls the club back. I force myself to stand still as he smashes it down past my shoulder and into the sideboard.

Immediately, he pulls the club up again. I take one last look at him, then I lead Hoshi away, through the kitchen and out of the back door. We tread round the rubbish and walk out of the gate and down the track, past the huddled cows and black fields. Our breathing fills the quiet night air and Hoshi holds my hand so tight that it hurts.

THIRTY-FIVE

We're too wired to go back to Hoshi's. Instead we buy chips and take them to the park. A few dog walkers stand by the gate, hands thrust deep in pockets, but the playground is deserted. We sit on the swings eating the hot salty chips, talking and swaying to and fro, our shadows drifting slowly across the ground.

'God,' says Hoshi, pressing her hand into her chest. 'My heart's still racing!'

'I'm sorry,' I say again. 'I told you he was crazy.'

'But you didn't tell me he'd be armed!' We laugh even though we both know there's nothing to laugh about. She turns to look at me. 'He scared me,' she says.

'I meant what I said. I think it was having you there.' I push a chip into the bottom of the packet, trying to get at the salt. I'm suddenly starving. 'But it's going to make him mad. I don't know what he'll do now . . .'

Hoshi's phone vibrates in her pocket, but she ignores it – it's been ringing on and off for ages – and pulls the zip of her coat up high. 'Tell me about him,' she says, passing me the rest of her chips.

'What do you want to know?'

'Everything.'

As I work my way through the chips, I tell her all about Alfie, starting right at the beginning when he'd bend back my finger if I moved his toys and I'd smack him in the face, giving as good as I got. 'Mum left us to it,' I say. 'She even got a book out of the library that told her to stay out of our battles. She said we were just trying to get her attention.' Hoshi blows on her fingers and my feet scuff the floor. I describe the tantrums he had if Mum tried to stop him from doing something he wanted to do and how he'd think nothing of throwing stuff at her too. How he got worse after Dad moved to Liverpool . . . and when he went to secondary school . . . and when he started doing weights. 'He's just got worse and worse,' I say. 'Only Gran could get him to calm down,' I say. 'Her and Alfie were close.'

'When did she go?'

'Two years ago. She went into a home. Then she died.'

The rest of the chips are cold. I roll up the packets and chuck them in the bin. Hoshi's phone vibrates again. She pulls it out of her pocket, checks the caller then turns it off. 'My agent,' she says.

'About the band?'

She nods. 'It's going to be called Happy Coco.'

'Oh my God!' I laugh. 'That's terrible.'

'I know.' She looks at me. 'Maybe Alfie will leave home soon.'

I shake my head. 'He's not going anywhere – no GCSEs, no job, no money. He wants to join the army, but they'll never have him. And I'm not going anywhere either. We're all stuck in that house together.'

'You could become a dancer,' she says, smiling. Her dimple pings on to her cheek.

I shake my head and pat down my pockets for a fag

that I know I don't have. 'I'll be lucky if I stay at school long enough to get my GCSEs.'

Hoshi starts to swing, getting higher and higher, leaning right back. 'You could do *anything* you want, Pearl.' She says this like it's the truth.

I let her words hang in the air, beautiful and exciting. Before tonight, I would have laughed at her, said something sarcastic, but could she be right? I never thought I'd stand up to Alfie, but I just did . . . For a moment, I let myself dream and I look way into the future. 'I'd love to be a dancer,' I say. 'Or be in musicals. I could be in *The Lion King*!'

'You could get paid to do the chicken noodle soup.'

'Yeah?' I smile and look out across the silent park and I start to wonder how that happens, what I'd need to do to make it come true. Mist hovers over the field where the dogs run and the trees are still and perfectly silhouetted.

Hoshi starts to swing higher and higher. 'We're the only people here,' she says. 'It must be late.'

And that's when I stop thinking about the future and

remember what's happening tomorrow. 'Hoshi, we need to practise your lines!'

She waits until her swing is at its highest point, then she jumps. She lands lightly and spins round. 'So let's practise!'

'What, here?'

'The fire truck can be the balcony.' Hoshi runs over to the climbing frame and climbs the rope ladder. 'C'mon,' she calls when she gets to the top. 'I need you to be Romeo.' She sits on the edge of the platform, her legs dangling. 'Do you know his words?'

I slip off the swing. 'I think I know the whole play.'

I go and sit on the cold ground below the truck, then I look up at Hoshi and say, '"See how she leans her cheek upon her hand."' Hoshi rests her chin in her hand and sighs dramatically. '"O, that I were a glove upon that hand, that I might touch that cheek!"'

'"Ay me!"' she says with a dreamy smile.

We work through the scene, stopping and going back a few lines if either of us makes a mistake. My fingers are so cold they're going white, but we don't stop. We want it to be perfect.

Hoshi's voice rings out in the night air. Far away, I can hear the distant hum of cars and a few lights shine through the trees. I look at Hoshi. Right now she does look like a bright angel, with her silver coat, blonde hair and background of stars.

'What?' she says.

'Distracted by the stars. There are so many tonight.'

She tilts her head back to look. 'We should go,' she says, her words misting the sky. 'It's late.'

'No,' I say. 'We need to finish this.' I get up, climb the ladder and sit next to her, our feet swinging side by side. '"I would I were thy bird",' I say, nudging her.

'"Sweet, so would I",' says Hoshi, nudging me back. '"Yet I should kill thee with much cherishing."' She turns to look at me. The air smells of bonfires and wet leaves. 'I always think Romeo and Juliet should kiss now,' she says.

Our faces are close. So close that I can see every eyelash above her deep, dark eyes. It's as though I'm seeing her for the first time: when she walked into the drama studio, jumped up on the stage and looked right into me.

'"I never saw true beauty till this night",' I whisper.

'That's the wrong line,' says Hoshi, then she puts her small cold hand on the side of my face, pulls me closer and kisses me, her smiling lips on mine, stealing my breath away.

I kiss her back.

I shut my eyes and melt in her smell of strawberry and mint. My body is alive, tingling to be so close to her. A distant bark, followed by footsteps, make us freeze, our lips barely touching. Hoshi breathes out and then our lips meet again and I never, ever want this to end.

Then the barking gets louder and we look up to see a dog dash across the park. The owner's nowhere to be seen. With a final bark the dog disappears. We look at each other for a moment, our faces lit up by the moon.

'Did you just kiss me?' I say.

Hoshi laughs and nods and I lie back on the platform and stare up at the sky, my mind dizzy, my heart pounding. Hoshi lies next to me, our shoulders touching. Our fingers entwine and a lightness spreads through my body. I stretch my free hand up towards the night sky and spread my fingers out. I'm amazed and suddenly I know that she's right: *anything* can happen.

I turn to face her, not sure how I can explain this. 'I feel like I could touch the stars,' I say.

She puts a silver arm across me. 'Me too.'

For a moment we lie in silence and I don't feel the cold. Being here with Hoshi feels so right that suddenly I never want to go home. I can't go back to creeping around my house, scared that Alfie will be in, scared about what he will do next. My throat feels tight and my chest aches. From nowhere, a tear runs down my cheek.

Hoshi's eyes go wide. 'What's the matter?'

I press my fingers into my eyes, almost surprised. 'I'm happy,' I say.

'You don't look happy.'

I laugh and cry at the same time. 'I'm happy, but I don't want to go back to my house. I *never* want to go home.' We sit up, but now I've started crying I can't stop.

'You can stay at my place,' says Hoshi. 'Dad will let you.'

I shake my head. I take a deep breath, then another and another. 'I could do that for a few days, but not forever.'

'We should go back to mine,' she says. 'Then tomorrow, before the show, we can go to your house. You can talk to your mum and tell her everything. Just like you said you would.'

I shake my head. Suddenly what I've got to do is as clear as the sky above me. 'Hoshi, I've got to speak to Mum. Right now.'

'Do it tomorrow,' she says.

'I need to do it while I still feel like this. Mum should be back soon. Right now I know I can make her listen to me.'

'Let me come with you.'

I jump down off the climbing frame and look back up at her. 'No. I've got to do this on my own.'

THIRTY-SIX

It feels like the farm is sleeping. I slip through the shadows, stepping round frozen puddles. Mum's car isn't back, so I open the gate, taking care not to scrape it along the ground, and peer in at the kitchen window. My eyes adjust to the darkness of the room. It's empty.

I let myself in and go into the living room, my shoes crunching over broken glass. It took a while to convince Hoshi that I would be alright, but in the end she realised she couldn't change my mind.

It looks like Alfie took all his anger out on Gran's picture of a horse sniffing a dog. He'll be in trouble. It's Mum's favourite.

Quickly, I send Hoshi a text telling her I'm back, and I'm fine, and that there's no sign of Alfie. Then I go down the corridor towards my bedroom. The door's open and that's when I remember.

I never locked it.

I push the door and it swings back. I hear . . . nothing. No bubble that tells me the pump is on, no hum that says the heater is gently warming the water. I don't want to turn on the light.

I stare into my moonlit room and gradually shapes emerge – jagged glass, cracks that span the width of the tank, sparkling diamonds on the waterlogged carpet.

Then, when I know what he's done, I reach for the light.

My beautiful tank is destroyed. The golf club Alfie used is still sitting in the gaping hole and cracks cover the remaining glass. The carpet is soaked with gallons of water and fish are scattered everywhere.

I look in the tank. A few fish are still swimming in what's left of the water, circling shards of glass. I count them – six – then rest the lid back on top.

My mind is numb, but I know what to do. I turn the central heating on constant and shine a lamp on the glass, hoping this will make the water warm enough to keep the fish alive. Next I pull the golf club out of the tank, then I kneel on the wet carpet and put the dead fish on a plate, side by side. I stack the broken glass on a spread-open copy of *Teen Vogue*, stopping every now and then to wipe away clinging strands of weed.

I'm trying to mop up water when I hear the front door open.

'Pearl?' Mum shouts. 'Alfie?' She walks into my room. 'What the hell's going on?' Her voice is furious, then she sees what's happened and her mouth drops open. I start picking up slithers of glass, dropping them on the magazine, peeling weed off my fingers. Then Mum's on the floor next to me, throwing my clothes to the side, helping me with the glass. 'Were you two fighting?' she says.

'No.' I sit back and try to pick at a splinter of glass that's stuck in the pad of my thumb.

'Let me do it,' she says, and she grabs my wrist. I look up at her. Her curly hair is escaping from a bunch and her mascara is smudged under her eyes. She holds my hand and tries to pluck the glass out, but her hands are trembling too much.

'I don't fight with him, Mum,' I say. 'He fights with me.'

'I've seen you wind him up.' She shakes her head.

My throat feels pressed tight. 'I wind him up by walking into the same room as him . . . By talking. By laughing. *By breathing*.'

Her face goes hard. 'Pearl, you're no angel —'

I snatch my hand away from her. It would be so easy to agree with her, but I won't do that any more. I point at the ugly mess of my smashed tank. '*This* isn't my fault,' I say. 'He *scares* me, all the time.' She sits back on the soaking carpet and looks down at her hands. 'I mean it, Mum. I can't live with him any more.'

'I know,' she whispers.

'You leave me alone with him . . .' She nods her head. 'You walk out when he starts on me . . . You even laugh when he does stuff!'

'I know,' she says, so quiet I can hardly hear her.

'Then why haven't you done something about it?' I

shout. I want to push her hunched shoulders, grab her. 'You're supposed to look after me!' She stares at me, eyes wide, then holds her head in her hands and cries. 'Stop it,' I say, because it's the worst thing I've ever seen. Her whole body is shaking and then she's howling. 'Mum . . . please!'

She looks around the room. 'Alfie did this?' Her voice is loud and ugly.

'Yes!' I say. 'You know he did it!'

She nods again, her face grim.

'Why don't you stop him?' I say.

'I don't know how to,' she says. She puts her hand on the side of my face. It feels strange, warm. She never touches me. I rest against it and shut my eyes. 'I'm sorry,' she says, pulling me to her and squashing me against her jacket. It smells of Chanel N°5 and horses. Ozzie's nose pokes my cheek, wet and hard, and she whines as Mum rocks back and forth, squeezing me tighter and tighter. 'I'm sorry . . . I'm sorry,' she says, again and again.

I've waited years for her to say this, but now I'm hearing the words, it's not enough. But I let her rest against me and cry into my hair because I don't know what else I can do.

We spend the next half an hour tidying up the mess. Mum alternates between crying and shouting at Ozzie. Suddenly she remembers that tomorrow is the opening night of *Romeo and Juliet* and she sends me to bed in her room.

I lie in the middle of her big, soft bed, Ozzie curled up on my feet. I keep the bedside light on. It used to belong to Gran and the rose-coloured shade makes the room glow pink. My eyes flick over familiar things that I haven't seen for a long time: bottles of nail varnish arranged on a glass tray, beads hanging on the dressing table mirror, Mum's black plastic jewellery box – the one that looks like a miniature wardrobe and is decorated with painted flowers. Everything is as carefully arranged as the rocks and plants in my fish tank.

Mum pushes open the door and sits on the side of the bed. The mattress creaks. 'You should be asleep,' she says. 'It's gone midnight.'

'I can't sleep.' She puts her hand on my shoulder, then takes it away. 'Where's Alfie?' I say.

'I rang him up. He's staying at Callum's.' I breathe into her pillow. It smells of her. 'I'm going to sort it out,' she says. 'I promise.' She leans over and switches off the light, but she doesn't go away. She sits on the bed and strokes Ozzie, occasionally stroking my feet as well. She tells me that tomorrow she's going to take me to World of Water and buy me a new tank, that we'll save the last six fish.

'I've spoken to Dad,' she says. 'He wants Alfie to go to his for Christmas, for a couple of weeks, then we'll work out what's going to happen next. He's going to go tomorrow.'

Alfie will be gone tomorrow? I start to drift off, wrapped in Mum's thick duvet, Ozzie heavy on my legs. 'I'm going to sort everything out,' Mum says as she strokes me, and I want to believe her so much.

Her hand squeezes my foot and Ozzie stretches out. 'Mum.' My voice is muffled by the duvet. 'I want to bring a friend round, show her the horses.'

'You could go for a ride,' she says. Then she starts telling me about a new route she's found over the Downs, but I don't hear what she says next because already my eyes have closed and I've let my mind wander back to the park, and the stars, and Hoshi.

THIRTY-SEVEN

I'm woken up by my phone. For a moment I don't know where I am, but then I see a photo of me and Alfie sitting on a pony, my arms round Alfie's waist, and I remember I'm in Mum's room.

I grab my phone. 'Hello?' but the call's been dropped. I notice how bright it is outside and realise I've been asleep for ages. My phone vibrates. It's a text from Ms Kapoor. **We need you at the theatre ASAP. Something has come up. x Ms K.** I jump out of bed and start to search for my leggings.

The door opens and Mum comes in carrying a mug of tea and a plate of toast. 'What are you doing?' she asks. 'I wanted you to have a lie-in.'

'Mum, can you drop me at the theatre?' I grab my

leggings off the back of her chair and pull them on.

'I suppose so.' She puts a mug of tea in my hand and I gulp it down. 'You'll burn your tongue. What's the rush?'

'I've got a message from my teacher. She needs me to go in early.'

'Why?'

'I don't know,' I say, staring at my phone. I've not had any texts or missed calls from Hoshi. I go to her number, but suddenly I'm scared to press it. Now the sun is shining and I'm back at home, last night at the park seems like a dream. I swallow as I remember all the calls Hoshi was getting. What if she changed her mind about the band? What if what we did, the kiss, made her want to run all the way back to Japan?

'What about your fish tank?' Mum asks.

'Mum, can you get it for me?' I'm panicking now, pulling my sweatshirt on, hunting around for my socks.

Mum folds her arms and stares at me. Eyes narrowed. 'What's going on, Pearl?'

'It's an emergency,' I manage to say. 'Please, Mum.'

She sighs. 'You'd better tell me exactly what you need. And write it all down.' She searches on her dressing table for a pen.

'Thanks, Mum,' I say, and I start scribbling a list on the back of an envelope. I know the stock off by heart. 'I've got some money saved up, but Jane will let me pay the rest back.'

'Slow down,' she says. 'I can't read your writing.'

'I need to get to the theatre.'

She passes me a plate of toast. 'Eat this first.' It's thin white bread, buttery and spread with jam. It reminds me of when I was little and off school sick. I sandwich the two pieces together. 'It always tastes best cut in triangles,' says Mum, watching me as I eat.

I walk into the auditorium and see Ms Kapoor on the stage with Mr Simms. They're standing in the centre of the stage, arms folded, too busy talking to notice me. 'It's not just a matter of finding a replacement,' Ms Kapoor says. 'We need someone who can dance.'

'And sing,' he adds.

'And who knows the script.' Ms Kapoor laughs and Sir puts a hand out to her. She grabs hold of it. 'We can't do the show,' she says.

My stomach squeezes tight and my legs wobble. 'Who do we need to replace?' I say, staring up at them. They spin round. 'Where's Hoshi?'

'Here!' says a voice behind me.

I turn round and there she is, wearing her Totoro hat with her My Little Pony hanging round her neck. Suddenly I love that My Little Pony! I want to hold her hands, hug her, but I don't dare. Instead, I just look at her and smile.

'What's the matter, Pearl?' She laughs. 'You look like you've seen a ghost.'

'You're here!' I say.

'Where did you think I'd be?'

'When you didn't ring I got worried,' I say. 'I thought you'd gone back to Japan.'

'You told me not to ring . . . And why would I go back to Japan?'

'To join Happy Coco.'

She shakes her head. 'I'm not going anywhere.'

'Girls,' calls Ms Kapoor. 'When you've finished chatting . . .'

We walk towards the stage. Our fingers link together. 'How did it go last night?' she says. 'I was so worried.'

I think about the mess in my room, the pile of dead fish on the plate. But then I remember waking up this morning and how the house felt like a different place, even though the living room was still full of dog food and there was a stack of dirty plates by the sink. 'I talked to Mum,' I say. 'Alfie's going to stay at Dad's.'

A smile spreads across her face. 'That's good?'

'Very,' I say.

'Girls,' says Ms Kapoor. 'This is important.'

'Tell me about it later,' Hoshi says. Then my fingers slip out of hers and we walk up the stairs that lead to the stage. 'What's happened?' she asks.

'It's Jake,' says Ms Kapoor, like it's obvious. 'He can't do the show.'

'What?' I say. Hoshi and I stare at each other. 'Why?'

'Rugby,' says Mr Simms. 'Last night he was helping with the juniors at his club when he broke his collar bone.' He shakes his head. 'He tripped over the ball!'

'And he definitely can't do the show?' says Hoshi.

'No way,' says Miss. 'He's in hospital right now. We need to have a think and see if we can replace him.'

'Because *somebody* thought we didn't need an understudy for Romeo,' adds Mr Simms.

'I was wrong.' Ms Kapoor sighs. 'There just weren't enough boys auditioning to find an understudy. I mean, there is Jonah . . .'

'Not Hairy Jonah, Miss!' I say.

'His hair isn't the problem,' she says. 'It's his singing.'

'I could work on his singing,' says Mr Simms. 'We've got all day. It won't be perfect, but –'

'It *has* to be perfect.' Ms Kapoor looks at her beautiful scenery. 'This is a professional theatre. People expect a professional production, not some dodgy school show!'

'So what?' I say. I can hardly believe this. 'We have to

cancel? All the weeks we've spent rehearsing have been for nothing?'

'None of us want this, Pearl.' She shrugs. 'But what choice do we have?'

'It's obvious what we should do,' says Hoshi. She's staring out at the auditorium, almost thinking aloud. She turns to face us, smiling. 'Let Pearl be Romeo.'

'What?' I burst out laughing.

'I'm serious,' she says. 'You know all Romeo's lines, you're an amazing singer and dancer –'

'But she's a girl,' says Mr Simms, speaking slowly. 'I know we've already switched a few of the male roles to female roles, but Romeo is the lead. *Romeo and Juliet* is the story of a boy and girl falling in love!'

'Why can't it be the story of two girls falling in love?' says Hoshi, looking at me. 'I think Pearl would make a great Romeo.'

Ms Kapoor is deep in thought, her eyes flicking between us.

'I suppose Shakespeare's plays were originally played by all-male casts . . .' says Mr Simms.

Suddenly, a big smile appears on Ms Kapoor's face. 'Hoshi's right. Why can't Romeo be a girl?' She laughs and throws her arms around Hoshi, wrapping her up in an enormous hug. 'You're a genius!'

Mr Simms flicks through the script. 'There's very little we'd actually need to change. Just swap the "he's" for "she's" . . . even the rhymes will still work in the songs.'

'Hang on,' I say. 'I haven't said I'll do it yet!' I try to get my head round what Hoshi's suggesting. 'So I'd be a girl called Romeo who falls in love with a girl called Juliet?'

'Exactly!' says Hoshi.

I walk to the front of the stage and stare out at the auditorium, at the rows and rows of seats stretching to the back of the theatre, and I imagine this actually happening: me walking on to this stage and speaking Romeo's lines, declaring my feelings for Juliet in front of hundreds of people. 'But who'd be Tybalt?' I ask.

'Me,' says Ms Kapoor. 'I know all the lines, the

fights . . . Plus the costume will fit me. But what do you think, Pearl? Do you think you can do it?'

I'm still gazing out into the auditorium. 'I think I can . . .' I say. But even as I start to believe this is something I can do, I'm filled with doubts. I turn round. 'What will everyone say when I walk onstage as Romeo?'

Ms Kapoor thinks for a moment. 'I guess that depends on *how* you walk onstage. Why don't you try something now?'

'Like what?'

'Any of Romeo's lines.' She gestures towards the theatre. 'See how it feels.'

I face the empty seats again and walk forward until my feet almost touch the edge of the stage. Below me is the orchestra pit, dark and cluttered with chairs and music stands. I take a deep breath then look up. '"I dreamt my lady came and found me dead –"' I say, my words ringing out in the vast empty space. '"And breathed such life with kisses in my lips, that I revived, and was an emperor."' For a moment the words hang in the air, then I realise how quiet everyone is behind me. 'So,' I say, turning round, 'what do you think?'

They're smiling and Ms Kapoor says, 'It works,' like she can't believe it.

'So, are you going to do it?' asks Mr Simms.

And I find myself nodding and I say, 'I'll be Romeo.'

THIRTY-EIGHT

I've spent so long watching Hoshi and Jake rehearse, I find it quite easy to remember Romeo's lines, sing his songs and know where to step. For the next few hours, Hoshi and I run through our main scenes, only stopping at lunchtime to share some sandwiches. Then, while we wait for the rest of the cast to come in, we focus on the songs. Ms Kapoor keeps telling me I'm doing great and Mr Simms can't believe it when I hit every note in 'Aint No Balcony High Enough' – 'Such a magnificent range!' he calls out.

We're practising our duet when the first cast members appear. Ms Kapoor tells them to sit in the auditorium while we finish, then she insists on giving us notes, ignoring all the curious faces watching us.

'Did you get that, Pearl?' Ms Kapoor says, tapping the script.

'What? Oh, yeah. Don't be too aggressive. Got it.'

'Just remember you're not Tybalt any more.' She looks up and sees that nearly everyone has arrived. She turns on the God-mic that's clipped to her top. 'As I'm sure many of you are aware,' she says, her voice echoing round the theatre, 'Jake has had to drop out of the show because of a rugby accident.' Talking breaks out and she holds up her hand until everyone is quiet. 'So that the show can go on, we've had to make some last-minute changes.'

I see Kat and Betty sitting in the front row. Bea and Bus Kelly are behind them. Along with everyone else in the cast, they stare up at me and Hoshi. 'As you can see,' says Ms Kapoor, putting her hand on my arm, 'Pearl has bravely stepped up and will be playing Romeo. Nothing has changed really, but our show is now going to be a love story about two girls.' Her words fill the silent theatre.

Suddenly, a single 'Yes!' bursts out from the front

row. I look up and see Betty jumping to her feet. 'Way to go, Pearl!' she shouts and she starts clapping. Everyone turns to stare at her and this just makes her clap even louder.

'Well, someone thinks it's a good idea,' says Hoshi quietly.

'*Betty* thinks it's a good idea,' I whisper back. 'That doesn't count.'

Betty's claps die out and Ms Kapoor says, 'What are you all waiting for? Get your mics on. We've got a show to rehearse!'

THIRTY-NINE

I'm not sure it's my fault the rehearsal is a disaster, but the moment I step onstage as Romeo, everyone around me starts forgetting their lines, calling me 'he' and walking in the wrong direction. The Year Ten boy playing my dad even misses his exit he's so busy staring at me, open-mouthed.

I, on the other hand, am pretty word-perfect. Even if I'm not Romeo-perfect.

The rehearsal is slow-going and some people find it difficult to adapt their lines at the last minute. Ms Kapoor is performing with us and keeps shouting out encouragement as she sings and dances. 'It's looking good,' she says as we get in our positions for the party scene.

'Really?' mutters Evie behind me. 'I'd say it's looking pretty –'

'What?' I say, spinning round.

She rolls her eyes. '*Good?*'

I turn back to face the front, shoulders tense. 'Smile, Pearl,' says Mr Simms. He's taken over the God-mic and is watching us from the orchestra pit, trying to conduct at the same time. I force my lips into a smile and stare at him until he looks away. 'OK, so straight into the party scene,' he says. Then he raises the baton to bring the band in.

I throw myself into the dance, but I know we're minutes away from the moment when Romeo and Juliet first meet, which also means we're minutes away from when Romeo and Juliet first kiss. Behind me are the rest of the company and I can feel their eyes burning into my back as we chicken noodle soup and dougie our way closer and closer to our first lines.

'"Villain"!' says Ms Kapoor in the first break in the music. '"I'll not endure her!"'

Then the music fades into the background and

everyone steps back; Hoshi and I meet in the middle of the stage and our hands lock together. As I speak my first line, Hoshi squeezes my fingers, trying to give me some of her confidence, but I know my voice needs to be so much stronger. Then it's her turn, and she's brilliant as usual.

We work through the scene and I try to take myself back to the park last night. I try to fill my words and movements with the confidence I felt when I was lying next to Hoshi, staring up at the stars – when I knew anything was possible – but I'm just too aware of everyone watching me: the cast, Chris at the prompt desk, the musicians in the pit. And I'm too worried about what they're thinking.

Hoshi pushes on. '"Saints do not move, though grant for prayers' sake",' she says.

'"Move not,"' I say, '"while my prayer's effect I take."' Then my lips brush the side of Hoshi's cheek, even though my heart is pounding just to be standing close to her, holding her hand.

'It makes my flesh tremble!' says Ms Kapoor, and I

feel like she's speaking for the whole company. Hoshi winks at me, then we're dancing again and I can relax, knowing that I'm finally doing something I'm good at.

We struggle on through the play, aware of how little time there is, until I'm kneeling by Hoshi's dead body, and I'm so eager to drink my poison and die that Mr Simms makes me come back to life and do it all over again.

Then it's over. All around me people grab bottles of water and some of them tell me how well I did, but I'm sure I can see the doubt written all over their faces.

'You've got half an hour until we need you back onstage for the sound check,' says Ms Kapoor, 'and then the audience will start arriving. We're sold out,' she adds. 'Grab something to eat then get changed.'

The stage empties, but the girls hang back. 'Can I just say,' says Bea, 'that you two were totally amazeballs!'

'Totally,' echoes Kat.

'Hoshi was,' I say. 'I was a disaster.'

'I'd say you were pretty good for your second ever rehearsal,' says Betty. 'You'll nail it tonight!'

'I hope so,' I say, then I walk to the front of the stage and twist up my hair as I try to cool down.

'Off you go,' says Ms Kapoor, ushering the girls off the stage. 'I need to speak to my leading ladies.'

Then it's just the three of us. I drop down on the floor and Hoshi sits opposite me. Miss looks around, checking there's no one in the wings, and I get the feeling I'm about to be told off.

'So, how did it go?' she asks.

'Badly,' I say. 'I was embarrassing.'

'No, you weren't,' says Hoshi, nudging me with her foot. 'You were amazing!'

Miss nods. 'Pearl, I do get why you feel self-conscious. We live in a small town and the show they are going to see tonight isn't quite what they're expecting. A few people might make comments –'

'*A few?*' I say, laughing, then I look out at the auditorium. I know Tiann is coming tonight along with a couple of hundred other students from school. What will they think when they see Hoshi and me kiss?

'*But,*' she says, 'you, more than most people, have the

power to make this work and to get everyone in the theatre cheering for you and Hoshi.' She pauses here and I study my hands, wondering just how much she's worked out about us. 'Just perform with utter confidence and everyone will believe in you.'

'I get it,' I say quickly.

'We'll be fine, Miss,' says Hoshi.

'Pearl?' says Ms Kapoor. 'Is this definitely what you want to do? Because now is the time to say if it isn't.'

I watch as a cleaner works his way along a row of seats, flipping each one down to check for rubbish. 'I want to do it,' I say.

'Take five minutes,' she says, dropping a bag by my side, 'but then you need to get ready.'

'What's this?' I look in the bag.

'Your costume. I bought two dresses for Hoshi because I wasn't sure which one she'd wear.'

She leaves us alone on the stage and I pull a black dress out of the bag. It's a skater dress, like Hoshi's, but off-the-shoulder. '*Kawaii*,' says Hoshi.

'Cute?'

313

'That's right.' All around us, the theatre is being prepared for the show. Voices call from the wings, props are dragged to the side of the stage and, up in the stalls, someone's doing some last-minute vacuuming.

Someone must be checking the lights because the stage is suddenly flooded with blue light. 'Hoshi,' I say, putting my face in my hands. 'I'm scared.'

Hoshi shifts round so that we're facing each other, legs crossed. She takes my hands in hers. 'Is it because of last night?' she says. 'I'm getting the feeling you regret it.' She laughs, but when I look at her I see that she looks as worried as me. We haven't spoken about what happened in the park. We've had no time on our own.

'No way,' I say, holding her hands tighter. 'I'll never regret that.' A spotlight swings across the stage, followed by another, then another.

'So why are you scared? You've been in loads of other shows. Why's playing Romeo going to be so different?'

'I was acting in those shows,' I say. 'It wasn't me . . . but what I'm going to do tonight is the most real thing

314

I've ever done!' I take a deep breath, then another, trying to stop the panic from rising inside me. 'At school, I've laughed at people who've dared to be a bit different; I've made their lives miserable!' I shake my head. 'Can I really stand on this stage tonight and say, "This is *me*. I've fallen for a girl. Please cheer for me"?'

We stare at each other. 'When Romeo goes to see Juliet on her balcony,' says Hoshi, 'how does he climb the wall into her garden?'

'Are you testing me?' I say. 'Because I do know my lines.'

She laughs. 'Just tell me!'

'He says, "Stony limits cannot hold love out."'

'There's only one way you're going to find out what people think about you falling for a girl: you're going to have to walk on this stage and see what happens, and you're not going to let anything stop you!' She holds my hands tight. 'You won't be on your own.'

A magenta light shines on us. I look into Hoshi's pip eyes. The light has made her hair pink, just like it was when she first walked into the drama studio and turned my world upside down. 'You're right,' I say, smiling. 'I can do this!'

'So let's get ready,' Hoshi says, jumping to her feet. 'We've got a show to do. Coming?' A bright golden light sweeps the stage. 'Pearl? We need to get ready!'

'You go,' I say.

'Don't be long.' Then I'm the only one left on the stage, all alone, staring at the rows of empty seats. A velvet curtain slides smoothly in front of me, brushing the floor and cutting me off from the auditorium.

'Pearl.' Chris, the stage manager, is standing over me, tapping his clipboard. 'You need to get your arse in gear.'

I smile up at him. 'I do, don't I?'

I let myself into dressing room one. It's next to the stage and we're using it to store our props. I work my way between the wheelie bins, bikes and skateboards until I get to the shower room. I lock the door and start running the water. Then I drop my clothes on the floor and step under the hot water. I lean my head back as spray hits my face and body.

I stand under the water for as long as I dare, knowing that I must be getting close to the sound check, then I wrap myself in a towel and pull the dress out of the bag.

I hold it in my hands. Out in the dressing room, the speaker buzzes, followed by the call, 'Ladies and gentlemen, sound check, please.' I hear giggles and footsteps as people pass the dressing room. I know I should rush upstairs, grab my mic and get back onstage, but I can't move.

I shut my eyes.

I hear water drip from the shower head and more people making their way to the stage. Then I open my eyes and stare in the mirror. Through the misty condensation, I see my bare face, my blue eyes and my dripping wet hair. I look at my pale eyelashes that I've got from my dad and the waves that are already appearing in my hair – my curly hair, just like Mum's and Alfie's.

More footsteps pass by outside, names are called and a shout bursts out. I put my fingers on the mirror and write 'Pearl' in the moisture on the glass. Mum once told me that wild pearls are extremely rare. A tiny speck gets into an oyster shell and is then transformed into a precious stone. I never used to like my name; I thought it didn't suit me.

It's quiet again outside. I step into the black dress and pull up the zip. It fits perfectly.

FORTY

'Have you been drinking?' says Betty, looking up from her iPod. Like Bea and Kat, her hair and make-up are done and she's already in costume.

'What?' I say. 'No!'

'Well, you look drunk.'

'Leave her alone,' says Bea. 'She's just smiling because she's wearing an awesome dress.'

'It does look good,' says Kat, glancing over. 'By the way, you missed the sound check and made Ms Kapoor say a very bad word.'

'I'll sort it out in a minute,' I say. 'Where's Hoshi?'

'She's ready. She's gone down to get a new mic,' says Betty. Then she peers at me. 'Where's your face gone?'

'No make-up,' I say. 'Stop staring, you freak.'

She laughs. 'That's more like it!'

Chris's voice rings out of the speaker. 'Ladies and gentlemen, this is your ten minute call. You have ten minutes. Thank you.'

'You need to hurry up,' says Kat. She's taken over the mirror and make-up is scattered around her.

'Who's got scissors?' I say.

'Me,' says Bea, passing me the pair of blue school scissors. She goes back to plaiting Betty's hair.

'Ow!' says Betty. 'You're hurting me.'

'Such a baby,' mutters Bea.

I gather my wet hair in a loose bunch at the side of my head and lean towards the mirror, nudging Kat aside. 'What are you doing?' she says, mascara brush suspended in mid-air. I start to cut my hair just above my fist. *Snip, snip, snip* go the scissors and my thick, tangled black hair falls around me. 'Oh my God . . .' Kat whispers, picking up a long strand.

'Pearl, stop!' shouts Bea.

But my scissors keep going. 'I'm sick of this stuff getting in the way.'

'Oh, wow . . .' Betty is smiling. 'Let me help.' She gets another pair of scissors out of her make-up bag and joins in.

'I think you'd all better help.' I pass my scissors to Kat and they gather round, tugging at my hair, arguing, snipping. 'Bea, can you take my nail varnish off.' I stick out my hands, then I watch in the mirror as they cut my hair into a bob that brushes my shoulders and my black nail varnish disappears.

The speaker crackles. 'Ladies and gentlemen, this is your five minute call. You have five minutes. Thank you.'

'Hairdryer,' I say and Bea blasts it into my face.

'Make-up?' asks Kat, approaching me with a fully loaded foundation brush.

'I'll do it,' I say, taking a blob of the foundation and rubbing it under my eyes and across my forehead. I add powder to keep off the shine. 'Vaseline?'

Betty hands me the pot and I dab some on my lips. She's still grinning and shaking her head. 'This might be the best thing that's ever happened in my life,' she says. 'I'm watching Pearl Harris get a make-under!'

'No way,' says Kat. 'The best thing was finding out Pearl was playing Romeo.'

Bea turns off the hairdryer and runs a brush through my hair while Kat starts to fix my mic in place, running the wire down my neck. Their fingers flick around me, pulling out strands of hair, snipping off the wonky bits.

'I think we're done,' says Kat.

They stand back and I look in the mirror, slowly turning my head from left to right. I run my hands through my hair, messing it up. 'Good,' I say. Then I smile. 'My head feels light.'

'Oh God!' Ms Kapoor is in the doorway, wearing my Tybalt costume. 'What have you done, Pearl?'

I walk to the middle of the room and the final call comes through: 'Ladies and gentlemen, this is your Act One beginners' call. All Act One beginners to the stage.'

I slip my mic into the pouch round my waist and smooth down my skirt. 'Just getting in role,' I say. 'How do I look?' I'm wearing hardly any make-up, no jewellery, no nail varnish, my hair is brushed away from my face and my shoulders are bare. I turn slowly round.

Ms Kapoor folds her arms and the girls' eyes flick from her to me.

'Honestly?' she asks.

I nod.

'You look like the best Romeo I've ever seen.' She smiles. 'Now off you go.'

We leave the dressing room and walk down the bright corridor. All around me, people stare, open-mouthed, nudging each other. 'Is that you?' whispers Bus Kelly.

'Boo!' I say and she laughs and blinks.

Evie gasps then covers her mouth, so I walk a bit taller as I pass her. I go down the stairs and then I'm in the passage that leads to the stage.

Kat catches up with me and puts her arm through mine. 'What's this all about, Pearl?'

'What? The haircut?'

'Everything,' she says.

We get to the wings and I stop walking. Betty and Bea join us. 'If I tell you, you'll laugh,' I say.

'Laugh about what?' says Betty.

'"Cousin, I do love a woman."' I say it loud and clear, just like I've always said things.

They look at each other as students push past us towards the stage. In the distance I hear the sounds that make my heart beat faster: the orchestra tuning up, the murmur of the audience, seats banging up and down.

'That's one of Romeo's lines from the play,' says Bea.

'But I mean it.'

'Can I just clarify?' says Betty. 'Do you love *women* or *a* woman?'

'Just the one.'

'Now this doesn't happen in *High School Musical*!' she says, laughing. 'Nice surprise, Pearl.'

I look at Bea and Kat. I have to know what they're thinking.

'I don't know why it's a surprise,' says Bea. 'I've known for ages that Pearl and Hoshi have a thing for each other.'

'You did?' I say.

'*Pearl and Hoshi?*' Kat sounds amazed. 'They have a thing for each other?'

Chris looks up from the prompt desk. 'Even I knew that,' he says. 'Now, keep your voices down.'

'It's more than a thing,' I say, looking right at Kat.

A smile spreads across her face. 'Well . . . Congratulations! She's a fox, Pearl.'

Now I'm smiling too. The orchestra has fallen silent and so has the audience.

'Group hug?' asks Kat, stretching her arms wide.

'No!' hisses Chris. 'No bloody hugs. Just get on stage!'

'Ladybirds,' says Betty, 'shall we do this?'

They leave me and walk on to the stage and get into their opening positions. All across the stage there are last-minute whispers, deep breaths are taken and glances are exchanged. Then, on an unseen command, everyone freezes. Bea is standing stage left, facing me. She smiles, tucks her thumb in and does the wave I invented so many years ago. Then I see Betty and Kat are doing it too.

I tuck my thumb in and wiggle my fingers back, then their hands fall down.

Beyond the curtain, the auditorium is totally silent.

I take a step closer to Chris at the prompt corner. In the monitor I can see the audience staring up at the stage. I search for my mum, but the picture is too grainy. Chris flicks on the offstage mic. 'For this evening's performance,' he says, his voice ringing out in the theatre, 'the role of Tybalt will be played by Kunnali Kapoor and the role of Romeo will be played by Pearl Harris.'

The picture may be grainy, but I can still see Mrs P in the front row, her eyes wide with surprise.

With a burst of sound, the orchestra starts to play, the curtain lifts and the lighting gets brighter and brighter. Onstage, it's the height of summer and tensions are simmering. With perfect timing, the cast swing to face the audience and break into 'Capulet It Go'.

On the opposite side of the stage, I see Hoshi step into the wings, her dress bright in the shadows. She stares at me, frowning, so I wave and mouth, 'It's me.'

She smiles and puts her hands on her chest. '*Sugoi*,' she mouths back. For a moment, we stare at each other as the cast slip in and out of our vision, fighting, dancing and singing.

'Pearl,' whispers Chris, beckoning me over. 'I need to check your mic before you go on. Give me a few words.'

'*Sugoi*,' I say. '*Sugoi, sugoi*.' He gives me the thumbs up then holds up two fingers, tapping at his watch. I stand ready in the wings. The street brawl is reaching its peak and the music is loud and frantic. The prince marches past me, yelling, '"Rebellious subjects, enemies to peace"!'

I shut my eyes and silently repeat my opening lines. *Is the day so young? Ay me, sad hours seem long . . .* again and again. When I look up, most of the cast are leaving the stage. Kat, Betty and Bea brush past me, patting my back, touching my arm. I force myself to breathe right down to the bottom of my stomach. I hope Mum is excited, staring up at the stage, waiting for me. *Is the day so young?* I repeat. *Is the day so young?*

Onstage, Benvolio says, '"See where she comes",' and looks in my direction.

I take another deep breath, then I step out of the shadows and walk to the centre of the stage.

There is silence.

Then I hear a voice asking, '"Is the day so young?"'

It's my voice and it is clear and strong. I put my shoulders back and I feel the warmth of the lights on my skin, then I raise my bare face to the audience and I gaze out like an emperor.